MIXED UP
WITH THE MOB

GINNY AIKEN

THORNDIKE PRESS
A part of Gale, Cengage Learning

GALE
CENGAGE Learning·

Detroit • New York • San Francisco • New Haven, Conn • Waterville, Maine • London

GALE
CENGAGE Learning

Thorndike Press® Large Print Christian Mystery.
The text of this Large Print edition is unabridged.
Other aspects of the book may vary from the original edition.
Set in 16 pt. Plantin.
Printed on permanent paper.

LIBRARY OF CONGRESS CATALOGING-IN-PUBLICATION DATA

Aiken, Ginny.
  Mixed up with the mob / by Ginny Aiken.
    p. cm. — (Thorndike Press large print Christian mystery)
  ISBN-13: 978-1-4104-0607-1 (hardcover : alk. paper)
  ISBN-10: 1-4104-0607-5 (hardcover : alk. paper)
  1. Large type books. I. Title.
PS3551.I339M58 2008
813'.54—dc22   2007051775

Published in 2008 by arrangement with Harlequin Books S.A.

Printed in the United States of America
1 2 3 4 5 6 7 12 11 10 09 08

. . . offer yourselves to God, as those who have been brought from death to life; and offer the parts of your body to Him as instruments of righteousness.

— *Romans* 6:13

ONE

Philadelphia, Pennsylvania

He'd never given marriage much thought. At least, not for himself. And especially not since God had seen fit to bless him with a grandmother like Dorothea Stevens Latham, a passionate and determined matchmaker. In fact, avoidance of the subject was one of David's favorite hobbies.

At the red light, he brought his vintage electric-blue Camaro to a stop, and watched a few snowflakes melt on the windshield. It hadn't felt all that cold earlier in the day, but years in Philly had taught him to expect anything from the weather. It was the twelfth of December, after all.

He flicked on his radio, and smiled at the sound of Miles Davis's mellow trumpet. It filled the car with its richness; it flowed over him like melted fudge. He loved music, especially the lushness of jazz.

The cell phone rang; he looped on his

hands-free headset. "Latham."

"So how was dinner with the lovebirds?" asked Dan Maddox, a fellow agent with the FBI's Philadelphia Organized Crime Unit.

The light turned green. David pressed the gas pedal. "Honeymooning agrees with J.Z., and Maryanne's just as radiant as on their wedding day."

"Wish I could've been there."

"Well, someone had to mind the store. Since I took the day off, and you are supposed to be on duty — oh, that's right. You're on 'sit and watch' detail."

"Yeah, yeah. I'm on surveillance. Don't rub it in. So how was dinner? Can the bride cook?"

David took the next turn. "You missed out, man. Homemade lasagna, garlic bread, the best green bean dish I've had in years and tiramisu. Eat your heart out."

Dan groaned.

David remembered how he'd felt the entire evening. Good food, good friends, good atmosphere. J.Z. and Maryanne's happiness had made a unique fourth at the dinner table.

And while his thoughts hadn't veered into dangerous territory during the visit, the minute he walked out of the cozy condo, a question had elbowed its way into his brain.

It didn't want to take a hike.

What would happiness like what he saw tonight be like?

How would it feel to close the door behind a visitor, and turn around to find himself in the company of the person who brought him that kind of joy?

". . . earth to Latham!"

He blinked. "Sorry. Guess I lost track of our conversation. I'm on my way to pick up Grandma Dottie."

"What's wrong with her brand-new Hummer?"

"Beats me. She just said it was in the shop, that she needed a ride home." Her request had stunk like a fine, tire-flattened polecat on a hot summer day. His grandmother was nothing if not independent.

But he'd rather discuss her than think of marriage. He muttered, "That only leads to danger, my man."

"Come again?" Dan asked.

David blushed. "Nothing. Just wondering what Gram's up to this time."

"Yeah, well. With her you can be sure she's up to something every time. Where is she?"

"I'll tell you, but don't you dare make any stupid comments, Maddox. She's at the latest Lady Look Lovely makeup party."

Dan's guffaws threatened David's eardrum. "Oh, yeah. She's up to something all right. She wants great-grandchildren, Latham, and she's lured you to an event peopled with women of all ages, sizes, shapes and interests. But there is one interest they all share, you know. Men, single men. Like you."

"That's not funny. I'd rather suffer bubonic plague than face that crew."

"Better you than me."

"Maybe that's what I should do. Have you pick her up. Sometimes I think she loves you better than she does me."

"Can't blame the woman for her good taste."

"Give me a break. Just for that, I'm gonna turn around and call her. Tell her I'm sending you in my place. You should face the 'sweethearts' she hangs around with. Especially those who aren't till-death-do-us-part attached to a sucker of the male persuasion."

With Dan's indignant squawks in the background, a niggle of discomfort crossed David's mind. That was how he'd viewed the lot of the average married man. Until tonight.

He murmured a few "Mmm-hmms" and a few "Huhs," which kept Dan happy and blathering.

David's thoughts ran rampant.

Maybe Dan *was* his best defense against Gram's zealous efforts, now that J.Z. and Maryanne had infected him with curiosity . . . and, if he were completely honest with himself, something he always tried to be, with a weird kind of emptiness in the pit of his — was that his gut that felt so jittery? Or was it his heart that made him feel strange, on edge?

He'd always thought the heart did nothing more than pump blood. He'd always rejected love-sloppy poets and schmaltzy chick flicks with their throbbing hearts and broken hearts and mended hearts. He'd always believed that the Lord would guide him to the woman he was meant to marry — *if* he was even meant to commit such lunacy in the first place.

". . . are you okay, David? I've never known you to space out like this, and you've done it twice now. You still driving?"

"I'm fine. Just irritated with myself. I can't help the soft spot I have for Gram. You should've heard her. She was in fine form this morning. 'Oh, Davey, it's not a problem. I'll just have Bea drive me home after the party. She only lives two houses down from me, you know.' "

Dan hooted. "Sure, as if we didn't know

11

that Bea Woodward has more driving citations than a stray mutt has fleas. I don't blame you. I don't want your grandmother careening down Philadelphia's wintry streets in that white-haired maniac's car any more than you do."

"And she knows how I feel."

"Too well." Dan gave another chuckle. "She's a special one, all right. But you're gonna have to brave the females and pick her up yourself. I'm on duty, remember?"

It was his turn to say, "Too well."

Four long blocks away from Lorna Endicott's palatial, old-money mansion, another red light made him stop. He tapped his fingers on the steering wheel, and "Uh-huhed" some more.

He sighed. How did Dad do it? How did the man handle such a mother? Was that why the moment he saw his chance back at the ripe old age of eighteen, his father bolted to the wild, wild West, and settled in Seattle?

Had that been the only way for Dad to find a mate on his own?

Maybe.

A car honked behind him, and David realized he'd been so caught up in his freaked-out thoughts, that he hadn't seen the light go green. He pulled forward with a jerk, his blush hot all the way to his forehead.

". . . you know why you're on your way to pick up Grandma Dottie. You're nuts about her. And I am, too — everyone is. She's the sassiest, sweetest, smartest woman I've ever met. And you'd do anything for your grandmother."

"I already admitted to my weakness, Maddox. So what's your point?"

"Just that I wish I could be there to see you face a crowd of women who just spent hours and beaucoup de bucks turning themselves into traps for unsuspecting guys."

At the next stop sign he looked both ways, relieved by the lack of traffic. True, it was ten o'clock on a Wednesday night, and he was driving down a posh residential neighborhood now, but you never knew when a speed demon would come at you with total lack of forewarning.

David tuned out Dan's teasing again, and started into the intersection. Headlights appeared in his rearview mirror. He wondered if it might be another sucker roped into an appearance at the Lady Look Lovely party. Maybe the two of them could commiserate —

A woman stepped into the crosswalk.

He honked, yelled, "NO!"

Dan's gibberish turned anxious.

The headlights pulled up to his left side. The gray Lexus roared ahead.

Twin beams limned the woman and a child she pushed behind. She stumbled on.

"Get off the street!" David yelled. He slammed the horn and stomped on his brakes.

Dan squawked some more.

David ignored him, tried to block the gray car with his.

The woman froze.

The Lexus swerved to avoid him then veered back, its aim sure, deadly. It hit her.

David skidded toward the sidewalk. "Call 911," he yelled at Dan. "Ambulance, too."

The car slowed. He gave Dan his location. Almost before he came to a full stop, David jumped out.

His temples pounded. He wanted to yell again, but something took hold of his throat. He rushed to the woman, who now lay on the road, the little boy frozen at her side.

An urgent prayer accompanied him down to his knees. "Are you all right?"

He took her pulse. Fast, too fast, but strong.

The woman, younger than he'd initially thought, gave him a wobbly grin. "Yes . . . no — maybe."

He forced a smile when he saw no blood. "Now there's a definite answer for ya."

"It's kind of hard to say. . . ." She worked her way up to a sitting position, her shadowed features twisted in pain. "I think everything's where it should be, and probably in working order, too. The car didn't hit me hard."

Her words contrasted with the fear in her eyes and the tremor in her hands. She held out her arms, and the boy crumpled into her embrace. Over the child's head, she met David's gaze. "Umm . . . you see —"

The boy's sobs cut her off. She turned her attention to the scared kid, who couldn't have been more than five or six. She murmured reassurances in a soft, musical voice, and her hands in turn dried tears, smoothed hair, checked for any sign of injury.

"He seems fine . . . right?" What did he know about kids?

She gave a tight nod. "The car didn't hit him. I made sure of that."

It struck him then that he'd failed to take note of the license plate on the Lexus. He made a face.

The woman inched away from him.

Great. He'd scared her. "Sorry. I just thought of something . . . important."

She scooted away a little more. "Please.

15

Don't let me keep you. I'm sure you have somewhere to go. We're fine."

Considering they were sprawled all over the middle of the street, David didn't agree. But she did have a point — one, only one. "That reminds me . . ."

He thanked the Lord for the lack of traffic, pulled his cell phone from his pocket, and dialed his grandmother. In a few, terse sentences he let her know an emergency had come up and that he'd be late. She knew him well enough not to doubt the tone of his voice.

As he turned back to the victims, he heard distant sirens. He breathed a sigh of relief.

"You're going to be okay," he told the frightened two.

The little boy's eyes looked like huge dark holes in the poor light. "You a doctor, mister?"

David grinned. "No, but my mother sure wanted me to be one."

The tyke frowned. "Did she make you time-out 'cause you dinn't 'bey?"

"No, not for that. But I spent hours and hours doing time-outs for all kinds of other things."

A spark of mischief rang in his "Really?"

"Don't bother the nice man, Marky. I'm sure he has to get going."

"Aunt Lauren! You know you shouldn't call me that."

The sirens wailed louder even than the boy's complaint.

Lauren tsk-tsked — nervously, to David's ear. "I'm so sorry, dear. Aunt Lauren forgot this time. It won't happen again. I promise."

Mark aimed narrowed eyes at his aunt. "Double-dip promise, with a cherry and whip cream on top?"

"Double-dip promise, with a cherry and *whipped* cream on top."

David was charmed, but not so much that he forgot what had to come next.

"Don't you think you'd better call his parents?" he asked. "The investigating officer will be here soon, and he'll want to ask you a million questions. The boy, too. The police will need parental permission to question him."

The smile the banter had brought to Lauren's face vanished. "Oh, dear. We don't need the police. I'm fine, and so is Mark. Nothing happened here."

"What do you mean, nothing happened here? That idiot ran right at you — and hit you! Then he pulled a hit-and-run. In my book that's two for one. Crimes, that is."

Alarm again filled her face. "Oh, no. Really. I'm sure the driver just skidded on

17

the wet pavement. It gets slippery when it starts to snow like this."

David snorted. "Look, lady — Lauren?" When she nodded, he continued. "The guy started out behind me. The minute you stepped into the crosswalk — on a green light for me, mind you — he hit the gas good and swerved around me. He was heading for you, and there's no other way to call it. This was no accident."

"You must be mistaken," she argued in a shaky voice. "It couldn't have happened that way. I'm sure it was the snow and . . ."

She stopped.

Shook her head.

Tightened her hold on Mark.

"Please," she whispered. "Send them . . . all of them —" she gave a little wave "— away. I'm fine. Nothing happened here. . . ."

Despite her urgent denials, David heard no conviction behind Lauren's words. Something wasn't right. Why was she so determined to avoid the paramedics and the police?

What had really happened before his eyes?

"Look, lady. I know what I saw. And I investigate crime for a living. My powers of observation are pretty sharp. So why don't you stop all this nothing-happened nonsense, and tell me what's coming down?"

"Nothing —"

"I'm a witness to your stepping into traffic *with a child*. I can press charges for child endangerment."

"No . . ." Her voice broke on a sob. "Please. I'm all Mark has left. His mother died three years ago, and it's only been three weeks since we buried my brother."

David gave a brief nod. "I'm sorry to hear that." He took a deep breath and withdrew his ID. "But that doesn't change what I saw. I'm with the FBI. Please tell me what just happened here, why you're so determined to avoid an investigation."

Another sob ripped through her. Fear left her features drawn, pale, eerie-looking in the weak glow of the streetlight on the opposite corner across the street. Unless he was much mistaken, her shivers intensified.

She began to shake her head.

He glared.

Mark reached up to pat her cheek. "You 'kay, Aunt Lauren?"

She tried to smile at the boy, but failed. "Fine, Marky. I'm fine."

"Lady —"

"My name's Lauren, Lauren DiStefano."

"Okay, Lauren DiStefano. I'm David Latham. Now why don't you tell me what you think happened here? What you *really* think happened here."

She took a deep breath, forced a . . . maybe she meant it as a smile, but from his point of view, it looked more like a grimace. She met his gaze.

"My brother's —" She shut her eyes, shook herself, then squared her shoulders. When she looked at him again, some corner of David's mind took note of her clear green eyes.

But it was her words that took him by surprise.

With a heavy dose of audible determination, she said, "My brother's *ghost* just tried to kill me."

Two

David rolled his eyes. "Let me get this straight. Nothing really happened here, you say. It was just a driver who slid on wet pavement. And that driver was . . . *your brother's ghost?*"

Lauren bit her lower lip. Then she squared her shoulders and nodded. "Yes. That's what I said."

But she didn't meet his gaze.

The ambulance shrieked up and came to a complete stop a few inches from David's feet. Two squad cars careered around the corner behind the siren-blaring, light-flashing, foot-threatening white-and-yellow menace. He scrambled upright, if for no other reason than to protect his feet.

But it was good. Reinforcements just when he needed them. He didn't know what to make of his accident victim.

Two officers approached. David nodded at them. "Glad to see you guys."

Officer Radford, as per his name tag, returned the nod. "Can you tell me what happened? The dispatcher wasn't long on details."

David withdrew his ID and turned it over to the two cops. "I was on my way down the street when a gray Lexus swerved around me and aimed straight at the woman and child. It hit and ran, and although she says she's fine, I think she might have a concussion or something. At the very least, she must've rattled her head."

The EMT who'd come up behind Officer Sherman, Radford's partner, waved her own partner toward Lauren then said, "Why her head? Did you see evidence of trauma?"

"No, but she's talking crazy."

With a puzzled look for him, the medic turned to Lauren.

Radford took out a notepad. "What do you mean, talking crazy?"

David snorted. "I feel stupid just telling you what she said. She tried to tell me her brother's ghost was behind the wheel. And that's after she insisted again and again that the driver had only skidded on the damp road."

Radford didn't look up from his scribbles, but his right eyebrow rose. "So we're talking criminal ghosts, are we?"

David ran a hand through his hair. He'd known better than to agree to come after Gram. Now he was making a fool of himself thanks to a pretty blonde who might have rocks in her head.

"That's what she said."

"Did you get a good look at the driver?"

"It happened so fast, I didn't even get a good look at the license plate, much less the driver."

"But you're sure it was a gray Lexus?"

"That I'm sure. My grandmother just traded in one just like it only in pink."

The eyebrow rose higher. "A pink Lexus. What'd she get? A pink Caddie instead?"

David's cheeks flamed. "No. A purple Hummer."

Radford's left eyebrow joined his right. He turned to Officer Sherman. "Is that ID for real, or did he get it in a gumball machine?"

Sherman scanned it again. "Looks plenty kosher to me."

David glared at Lauren. "Call the office. I'm for real. I'm just not sure what she is."

"She," said the female EMT as she returned, "is just fine. Oh, she'll have a doozy of a bruise on her hip by tomorrow, all right, and I'll bet she scraped her knees good under those pants, but otherwise she's fine.

23

Not even a bump on her head."

"Then she's nuts," David said before he could stop himself.

Lauren glared back. "I'm not crazy, but I am fine, as I told you over and over again." She turned to Radford. "He shouldn't have made such a fuss. I'm sorry he bothered you, sir. But as you heard, I'm fine. You can all go home now. It's getting late, especially for my nephew."

Radford glanced at David. In that quick look, he saw the same alarm he'd felt at Lauren's urgent objections. Something was up with this woman. And he wasn't about to let her go until he had a good idea what it might be.

David crossed his arms and pinned Lauren with his stare. "Listen. I don't buy a word of your ghost story, so why don't you try telling me the truth? What's going on here? What are you trying to hide?"

At his side, Radford cleared his throat.

David winced. He was stepping on the locals' toes, and he was off duty, but by now he'd lost his patience. He had to know what Lauren DiStefano was up to.

Instead of answering, though, she helped her nephew stand before she stood, as well. Only then did she meet David's gaze. "I'm sorry. I'm absolutely exhausted. And I've been under a great deal of stress these last few weeks. I'm sure it's all taken its toll on my sanity."

David caught himself before the spontaneous "Yeah, right" popped out. "So in your world exhaustion and stress lead to hit-and-runs and ghosts."

She had the decency to blush. "I suppose it does sound stupid when you put it that way."

"What way would you rather I put it?"

The shrug made her wince. She was hurt, no matter how hard she tried to deny it. What he wanted to know was why she was so determined to do so.

"Well?" he prodded.

Radford's pencil scratched across paper.

The ambulance pulled away, this time minus the theatrics.

Officer Sherman joined them.

Still, Lauren didn't speak. By now, she'd grown visibly uncomfortable with the triple scrutiny — just what David had hoped for. Maybe that discomfort would make her decide to talk.

She took a deep breath, clasped her nephew's shoulders, pulled the boy close to her side. "The last three weeks have been very hard on us. My older brother Ric died twenty-three days ago. A car accident."

That did explain stress, and the stress probably explained the exhaustion.

"But how do we get from grief and mourning to a Lexus-wielding ghost?" he asked. "Are you sure your brother's dead? That you didn't . . . uh —"

"No, Mr. Latham," she cut in, her green eyes bright with indignation. "I didn't imagine my brother's death. I could never have done that. Besides, I have plenty of evidence of his passing."

"I didn't mean that you might have imagined his death." David shifted his weight from one to the other foot. "That evidence you mentioned would be . . . ?"

"The usual," she countered. "I have a death certificate, the obit from the newspaper, the tasteful gravestone I had to order, a casket and fresh burial plot, the unending funeral bills I still have to pay and none of those is even the most heartbreaking bit of proof you could ever want. I have a grieving five-year-old nephew who only wants to know where his daddy went."

David's gaze dropped to the boy. The tears in Mark's large green eyes, so like those of his aunt, filled him with guilt. "I'm sorry. I probably shouldn't be asking these questions with . . . ah . . . him here."

"You shouldn't be asking them period,"

she said.

"Amen," added Radford.

Although their objections didn't have the same meaning, David got where they were coming from. He shot the cop an apologetic glance, but then his attention flew back to the woman and child in the blink of an eye. "Maybe you shouldn't be talking ghost stories, either."

To his satisfaction, she glanced down at the boy, and frowned. "You're right. I'm going home."

"Not so fast, lady," Radford said. "I need your name, address, telephone number, and the full name of that maybe-dead, maybe-not-so-dead brother of yours."

David didn't let his gaze stray as Lauren responded. But then, when she got to her brother's name, a touch of recognition tickled the backside of his memory.

Ric DiStefano.

He knew the name. But he couldn't quite place it. Not right away, at any rate. He'd have to think about where he'd heard it, how he came to know it.

Then, to his surprise, after Radford's okay, Lauren walked to the large, three-story brownstone mansion two doors from the corner, unlocked the door and slipped inside. She lived *there* and she complained about funeral bills?

Something still didn't add up.

While he stared at the double mahogany doors, someone tugged on the back of his shirt. He turned around and groaned.

"You okay, Davey?" his grandmother asked.

Oh, boy. Was he ever in trouble now! His grandmother at the scene of a crime.

"I'm fine, Gram. What are you doing here?"

"Sure you're fine?"

"Yes, I'm sure. So why are you here?"

At nearly six feet of statuesque height, Dorothea Stevens Latham rarely looked anything but her usual competent, eccentric self. Right now, though, under the weak glow of the streetlight at the other corner, his grandmother looked shaken.

Guilt filled him. He opened his arms wide, and she stepped into his hug. He felt her shivers in the deepest corner of his heart.

"Aw, Gram," he said as he patted her sturdy back. "You shouldn't've worried. I'm fine. It's just that I witnessed a hit-and-run."

Then she shuddered, took a deep breath, and stepped away. "And just how was I supposed to know that, David Andrew Latham?"

Now this was more like it. "Because I

called you and told you Dan would pick you up. Then I bet he told you the same thing."

She tossed her head of snow-white spiked hair. "Well, Davey dear, I like Danny just fine, but he's every bit as much of a spook as you are. How'm I supposed to know when he's telling me the truth and when he's feeding me Bureau gobbledygook?"

"Ahem," said the alluded-to spook. "I'm not given to lying, Grandma Dottie."

David's friends all wound up adopting his grandmother as their own. The world's very own professional grandmother turned to Dan Maddox. Her canary-yellow full-length wool duster coat swirled around her.

"Maybe not, Danny, but you'll be the first to bend the truth to cover for Davey or any of your other fellow agents. And you can't deny it."

Dan met David's gaze. The two men exchanged a knowing look. There wasn't much either could say to the older woman. She knew them too well.

"So I'm right, then," she continued. "Not only did I have to come see that you really were in one piece, but I also had to check to make sure you hadn't cooked up a goofy excuse to not come and pick me up. I don't know what you have against my friends. They're such lovely gals."

Now she'd started in with her guilt-inducing poor-me deal. "Hey, Gram, give it up. You may as well quit while you're ahead. I'm not buying that 'what you have against my friends' stuff. You know I don't have a thing against your friends. I just have a problem with your devious ways. I can find my own dates, you know."

She snorted. "Well, you're doing a lousy job of it, if you ask me. And I know some swell girls."

"Well, I didn't."

"Didn't what?"

"Ask you."

Gram stuffed her fists in the pockets of her outrageous coat and pushed out her bottom lip.

Now, really. Who else wore nearly neon-yellow in December?

Who else wore nearly neon-yellow at any time?

She lowered her head.

Anyone else would've thought she was contrite. Not David. He knew she was busy scrambling in her troublemaker brain for another plan of attack.

It was time to deflect the skirmish. "Well, listen —"

"So did you get the pretty blonde's number?" she asked.

Without thinking, David said, "Her name, address, phone number . . ."

At the gleam in his grandmother's brown eyes, David let his words die a merciful death. She'd tricked him well and good.

"Is there any reason to think this rises to the level of a Federal situation, Latham?" Radford asked.

David had forgotten the officers. "Ah . . . no. I doubt it."

Sherman nodded. "Then we'll take it from here. As a courtesy, we'll let you know if we learn anything different than what we know now."

"That's fine. And thank you for your quick response. I appreciate it."

Radford chuckled. "At least someone does. It doesn't look like Ms. DiStefano thinks much of us."

David glanced at the expensive house down the street. "Don't take it personally, Officer. It strikes me that she doesn't think much of law enforcement period."

"I'm with you," Sherman said.

"D'you mean that pretty girl?" his grandmother asked. "Are you boys saying she's a crook?"

Her disbelief struck David as somewhat naive, but he didn't have much to go on. "No, Gram. We have no evidence that she's anything but what she says she is — a grieving sister who's been left to raise a miserable little orphan boy."

"So where's the but?"

Nothing much got past her. And she wouldn't let up on him until she learned what she wanted. So he said, "But something's not quite right about that ghost story."

"What?" she squawked. "Don't tell me she's one of those séance-happy nuts. She sure didn't look like one."

"And just how do people who're into all that spiritist junk look, Grandma?" Dan asked, humor laced through his words.

Grandma Dottie shrugged. "Oh, the ones I've seen on talk shows wear yards of filmy fabric, too much eye makeup, and talk like spaced-out teenagers. And they haven't been teens for decades, you know."

David had a sudden vision of a well-upholstered matron, a cloud of lavender chiffon in swathes around her . . . upholstery, raccoon-black goop around turquoise-shadowed beady eyes, her hair a perfect Miss Clairol shade of champagne and giant gobby rings on her every finger.

"That's it," he said. "It's late enough that my mind's begun to do a Grandma Dottie meld. Reality check, folks. And time to head home." He turned to Dan. "Hey, thanks for everything, man."

Dan chuckled. "Are you kidding? I live for this kind of thing. I called Eliza, told her what was up with you, and what wasn't happening at my post, and she couldn't send me after you fast enough."

"Great. Now I'll have to face the dragon lady first thing tomorrow morning."

"Make sure you have your Wheaties," Dan said with a wink. "You gotta walk into the dragon's lair well fortified, you know."

"First ghosts, and now dragons," David said. "Let's go home, Gram. You can tell me what's wrong with your Hummer on the way."

He drove the short distance to his grandmother's elegant town house in a historic district of Philly only half listening to her tale of Hummer woe. To his disinterested ear, it all sounded like a cooked-up excuse to drag him to the cosmetics party, after all. And that didn't particularly bother him. He knew his grandmother very, very well.

He didn't, however, know Lauren DiStefano at all. But he did know he was going to get to know her a whole lot better. And soon.

Because he'd just remembered where he'd heard the name Ric DiStefano. DiStefano was a big-time venture capital guru.

And his business, DiStefano Enterprises, was under investigation for SEC violations. It'd been all over the news. To make matters worse, it seemed the guy'd had possible connections with Mat Papparelli, a dead money launderer for the mob.

A late mobster whose widow had turned state's evidence. The very same woman Dan Maddox was supposed to be keeping in protective custody.

Why would Eliza Roberts, Dan and David's boss, pull Dan from his assignment? Why would she send him after David's ghost-loving hit-and-run victim?

Organized crime was David's shtick.

What was Lauren DiStefano's game?

THREE

"What's this about ghosts, Agent Latham?"

David looked at Eliza Roberts, a brunette knockout with blazing green eyes. "Trust me, Eliza. There's nothing to it. But something's up with that DiStefano woman, and I'm going to find out what it is."

"Good. Because as of now, she's all yours."

He gave her a nod. "Thanks. I was pretty sick of pushing papers between real jobs."

She smirked. "Can't keep you field guys in one place for long, can I?"

"Do you really want to?"

"Someone's got to keep up with your paperwork, and no one can read what you guys call writing. But I'll admit it's a waste of manpower when you sit around for too long."

That comment didn't sit very well with David, but he knew better than to call her on it. Eliza Roberts was not one to mess with.

"What's the scoop on Ric DiStefano?" he asked instead.

Her superior smile got under his skin. She wasn't very likable.

"Here's the file we have on him."

The slim manila folder landed right in front of him on the vast expanse of polished wood. The Bureau didn't provide such luxuries, not even for their Supervising Special Agents. The desk's provenance, as well as that of Eliza's pricey leather chair, was the subject of much speculation in the office.

"Not much here, is there?" he asked after he leafed through the few sheets.

"What you see is what you get. We got a heads-up from the SEC guys about six weeks ago. That's what they faxed us."

The tight electric rush he got at the start of an investigation zipped right through him. "So it's a fresh one. Is anyone else on it?"

"No. I saw no reason to assign it. From where I stood, it looked like a typical SEC case. They'd just copied us on it because of the possible organized crime connection. I'm sure if they'd found more, they would have sent it on. And the connection looks pretty weak to me."

David gave her a skeptical look. "Then

why'd you send Maddox over last night?"

She turned to avoid his gaze — or so it seemed.

"He wanted to go," she said. "And he said something about picking up your . . . grandmother. That doesn't sound right, does it?"

"Maybe not, but yeah. I was on my way to pick her up when the deal with Di-Stefano's sister came up. I'd been on the cell phone with Maddox, and I asked him to call 911 and to make sure she got home safe. And, sure, he did call 911, but then he also showed up at the scene."

Alarm filled Eliza's face. "But not with an elderly woman, right?"

"Sorry. Maddox brought her along."

"What was he thinking? The cops had a hit-and-run and a five-year-old child to contend with. And Maddox went and made matters worse by bringing a frail senior citizen to the scene?" She shook her head. "I'm going to have to talk to him —"

"Don't bother," David said. "My grandmother's anything but fragile. She's nearly six feet tall, built like a battleship, has the instincts of a fox and the nine lives of a cat. She was in no danger. Believe me."

Eliza's frown didn't ease. "That was a serious lapse in procedure, Latham. And you know it. Maddox does, too."

"Cut him some slack, will you? I asked him to take care of my grandmother, and you sent him to a scene that was already under investigation by Philly's best. I was there, too. Why would you want to divert Dan's attention from his merry mob widow?"

Again, Eliza's green eyes danced away from David's gaze.

His instincts weren't much shabbier than Gram's. Something was happening. And Eliza knew it as soon as Dan called to tell her what David had witnessed. He doubted she'd had the gray Lexus under surveillance. That only left one other possibility.

"Why are you keeping tabs on Lauren DiStefano?" he asked.

Eliza jerked around to face him. He'd hit the nail on the head.

"I suppose I can tell you now that I've assigned you to the case," she said. "We've been watching the house since the tip from the SEC. As soon as Maddox told me where your accident happened, I figured another pair of eyes wouldn't hurt."

"So why keep it a secret from me? As you said, you did just assign me to the case."

She shrugged. "Habit, I guess. I like to play things close to the vest."

David snorted. "Maybe too close. Either you give your field agents all the info, or you wind up with a mess, maybe even egg on your face. We can't operate in the dark."

She tipped up her chin. "Are you trying to tell me how to do my job, Agent Latham?"

He rolled his eyes. "I wouldn't presume."

She narrowed hers. "Good. Keep it that way."

David took her response as dismissal. He went toward her office door. "I'll be in touch."

"Yes, you will. And one more thing, Latham."

"What's that?"

"Just see that you don't pull a stunt like J.Z. on the Papparelli case, will you?"

He faced her in slow motion. "What do you mean by that?"

Eliza placed her hands on the top of her desk and locked her emerald gaze with his. "No fraternizing with the enemy . . . the subject of the investigation."

In a flash, Lauren's frightened face burst in his memory. Her clear green eyes, so different from the dark, unreadable emerald ones of the woman before him, seemed to reveal everything inside her.

Fear.

Horror.

Confusion.

Up until then, David hadn't realized the strength of the pull Lauren DiStefano exerted on him. And J.Z.'s and Maryanne's wedded bliss had nothing to do with it.

He left the office without another word.

At nine o'clock the next morning, Lauren dragged her sore, creaky body out of bed. The long soak in the Jacuzzi tub and the four tablets of ibuprofen hadn't helped one bit. She felt as though the proverbial Mack truck had rolled right over her — twice.

The house was quiet. More than a hundred years ago the builders had made the walls so thick that they insulated the occupants from all outside sound. That was a blessing.

On the other hand, so much silence could also mean trouble. She did share the place with a normal, mischievous five-year-old. No noise often offered warning of a disaster in the making.

With great reluctance, she pulled her silk robe over the matching pajamas, and made herself walk the short distance to Mark's bedroom. He could still be asleep. After all, they hadn't made it to bed until well past midnight.

She opened the door and sighed in relief. The boy's slight body lay right where it should be, on the custom-built racecar bed he loved.

Poor kid. He'd lost his mother to leukemia three years ago. Then Ric died in that horrible wreck. And now, he'd gone through the shock of a near miss with an out-of-control car. It was a miracle the child could sleep at all.

She closed the door and went downstairs. She needed coffee, a double-shot espresso, at the very least. Maybe then her blood would start to circulate. Something had to oil her beat-up muscles. She couldn't waste a whole day on the old fainting couch in the library like some wilting lily from the Roaring Twenties.

Even though the aches and pains tempted her to do just that.

At the professional stainless steel machine, she poured roast beans into the grinder, buzzed them into fine powder, then pushed the appropriate sequence of buttons, and watched the contraption do its thing.

Her brother had been so proud of his espresso maker. "It's just like the ones they use at Starbucks," he'd said the day he'd had it installed.

She felt a pang of sadness. Ric hadn't been

able to enjoy it for long. Three months after installation, during which he'd been out of town on business more than once, he was gone.

The luscious scent of fresh-brewed coffee filled the enormous kitchen. Lauren didn't like the room's sterile whiteness, but she did appreciate the high-end appliances and the extreme convenience the appointments provided. And she did love to cook.

She took her cappuccino cup — the double-shot didn't fit the thimble-size espresso cups Ric had imported from Italy — to the table. From the jar on the marble countertop, she took a large, anise seed biscotti then plopped in a chair. After a few sips of rich java and crunches of crisp biscotti, she began to feel more like herself.

Not good.

The memories of last night flooded in with a vengeance.

That silver car had gone straight for her. And she did get a good, clear look at the driver.

If that hadn't been Ric at the wheel, then it had to have been his ghost come back to haunt her.

But she didn't believe in ghosts. She never had. Not any more than David Latham did. *FBI Agent* David Latham.

42

He'd made no secret of his suspicion. But there was nothing she could say. She had no idea how or why Ric — or his ghost, the one that didn't really exist — would have wanted to run her down.

"Aunt Lauren?"

She shook herself. "I didn't hear you come into the kitchen, honey. How'd you sleep last night?"

Mark crawled up into her lap. "Good."

When he laid his head on her shoulder, her heart melted. She gave the Lord silent thanks for the boy's safety. She didn't know what she would have done had he been injured last night.

That had haunted her dreams.

"Are you hungry?" she asked.

"Mmm-hmm."

"What would you like? Cereal or waffles?"

"Awfuls. With whip cream."

Lauren smiled. Normally, she would have corrected him, but not today. Today his little-boy talk seemed even more precious than ever.

"Okay, then. Awfuls it is." She rubbed his dark curls. "And how about juice? Orange or grape?"

"Great's my favorite."

She hummed a few bars of the old song about the Purple People Eater. Mark giggled. Just as he always did.

The normalcy of the moment helped set her fears at bay. But she knew it was just a temporary reprieve. Something had happened last night. Something terrible. And she didn't know why.

But she had to find out.

If not for her sake, then for the sake of the child she loved so much.

"Wanna watch my shows, Aunt Lauren."

"Sure thing, kiddo." She grabbed the remote and clicked on the children's educational program Mark liked. She pulled out ingredients and mixed batter for the waffles. She sprinkled water to test the heat of the electric waffle maker, then spritzed it with nonstick spray, and finally poured the thick mixture onto the distinctive, ridged surface.

The scent of food made her stomach rumble.

As she withdrew a plate from the warming drawer where she'd put it five minutes earlier, the doorbell sang with the Westminster chimes.

"Whozzat?" Mark asked.

"Good question." Lauren wasn't expecting company. And no one she knew would just show up so soon after a death in the family.

"Only one way to find out, kiddo."

Mark nodded, his attention on the television set.

"Stay here, okay?"

He nodded again.

"I'll be right back."

" 'S okay, Aunt Lauren. Go on."

She headed toward the front of the house, a smile on her lips.

A smile that died when she looked out the tiny round peephole.

The stranger on the front stoop didn't exactly give her a case of the warm fuzzies. Although he was well dressed in an expensive-looking charcoal summer-weight wool suit, his hard-set features and brooding gaze alarmed her.

She'd just about decided to pretend she wasn't home, when the guy rang the bell again. The melodious chimes were followed by pounding.

"I know youse in there," he said, his voice a low growl. "So open up already."

With a prayer for protection, Lauren opened the door — but only as far as the chain on the lock would let her.

"Yes?"

The man looked startled. "Oh. It's you."

It was her turn to be surprised. "Of course, it's me. I live here. Who're you?"

His chin, just shaved but already darkened

by the regrowth of heavy beard, jutted. "So where's your old man?"

"My old man?"

"What's wrong with youse? Can't you hear right?" He shook his head. "Where's Ric? Last time I spoke wid him he told me to be here by ten. And no one can say ah . . . er . . . Boris Martinez is ever late."

A spooky feeling overtook Lauren. Boris Martinez had talked to Ric. And what kind of phony, cooked-up kind of name was Boris Martinez, anyway? Who really was this guy? "You . . . you talked with Ric?"

He muttered something.

She was glad she didn't quite catch it.

"That's what I said, ain't it? I talked to Ric, and he told me to be here by ten. I'm here, and you ain't him. So where is he?"

Tears filled her eyes. Too many emotions to identify any one ripped through her. Lauren closed her eyes for a moment, prayed for help, for peace, for this horrid person to leave her alone.

"Ric's dead, Mr. Martinez."

That shocked him. After a few moments of slack-jawed surprise, he clamped his mouth shut and narrowed his gaze. "How can he be dead, lady? I just talked to him . . . oh, not three weeks ago. And I woulda heard if someone'd —" He stopped, cleared his throat. "I woulda heard if something'd happened to him."

Lauren had had it with her unwanted visitor. "Well, something *did* happen to him. Three weeks ago, as a matter of fact. And it doesn't matter whether you heard about it or not. My brother died in a car accident twenty-four days ago, Mr. Martinez. Now, if you don't mind, I have a lot to do. Good-bye."

He stuck the pointed toe of his hand-sewn leather shoe in the crack between the door and the frame. "Not so fast, lady. I don't believe a word you said. Ric DiStefano ain't dead. And you better not try and pull a fast one on me. He owes me a whole pile of dough. And he ain't about to stiff me by pretending he's stiff — you get my drift?"

All she wanted was for him to leave. So she said, "Fine. I'll be sure to tell him the next time I see him. At the cemetery, when I go put flowers on his grave."

"We'll see about that grave thing," he groused.

Lauren looked down at his fancy footwear, then, with determination and total disgust, she did what she should have done at the start. She shoved her foot against his, dislodged it enough to gain a scant advantage, and shut the door.

47

Despite the house's heavy construction and the thick wooden door, she heard his objections all the way to the kitchen.

If he didn't leave in the next five minutes, she was calling the cops. No matter what.

Because now she realized that the deer-in-the-headlights feeling she'd experienced last night had been no accident. Something was going on. Something dangerous. Something she didn't like.

And she wasn't going to just sit and take it.

She was going to find out what was what.

Lauren didn't know how or why she knew it, but she did know her life depended on what she learned. Worse yet, Mark's life depended on it.

And no one was going to hurt that little boy.

No matter what.

FOUR

He'd been too tired to drive home after the accident, so David spent the night at his grandmother's. He benefited from the vast, luxurious bed he used when he stayed with her, and in the morning she greeted him with one of her "groaning board" breakfasts — two juices, apple and grapefruit, pancakes and real maple syrup, eggs, ham, sausage, bacon, coffee, tea and two kinds of sweet breads.

No way could he eat like that and hope to put in a decent day's work. So his reasonable serving brought about the expected commentary.

"Are you all right, Davey? You've hardly eaten a bite. You sure you didn't get hurt last night?"

"I'm fine, Gram, and it's way past time you stopped calling me Davey. You know it."

She winked. "Sure. But it's so much fun

to bug you. I love to see you blush."

"You're a sadist, you know that?"

"Nope, not at all. I'm just your grand-mother, and teasing you is fun! You'll get it when you're a grandpa yourself — and you know that."

Over the years, David had learned to ignore certain of his grandmother's comments; the grandpa one was classic Grandma Dottie. "Okay. So we both know you love to tease me. How about we skip the Davey deal, since we both also know it's so hokey?"

She spread her intense purple-draped arms. "This is my home. When you're here, I get to bug you all I want. When we're at your place, you get to bug me all you want. Isn't that fair?"

"Listen, you sly fox," he said with a chuckle. "You'd better add something about when we're in public to your oh-so-generous offer. I didn't catch anything about those times."

She pouted, then waved. "Public, schmublic. You'll just have to wait and see. That's all I'm going to promise."

He gave her a mock scowl. "Be that way, then. But I've got to go. Some of us have to work."

She erupted like a purple satin and gold

lace volcano. "Don't give me that, buddy boy! Sure, your grandpa inherited the house and a little bit of money, but then the two of us worked mighty hard for decades to turn that little money into enough to give back to the Lord for what He'd given us and to provide for our family. And you know I still operate that way."

He raised his hands and blushed. "That wasn't at all what I meant, Gram, and if that's how it came across, I apologize. Please forgive me for the dumb statement."

"Of course, I forgive you, David." Her tight hug filled him with a shot of pure love. "And I'm sorry I took offense. Now, go! Get yourself to work with the rest of your pals."

On the way to the office, he had to deal with the sloppy streets. It was early enough, cold enough and wet enough that last night's slush hadn't melted but was enhanced with more of the same. If the thermometer dipped even a couple of ticks, the streets would turn wicked. He hoped the salt trucks came out in hordes.

The elevator to his floor crawled up at its usual slow pace. When it finally got there, he grabbed a cup of what they dubbed FBI sludge from the nearly empty coffee machine and went straight to his desk. After the bitter brew scalded his tongue, he sat back, then closed his eyes.

Ric DiStefano.

He'd scanned the file Eliza gave him, and the pathetically few facts he found there made him wonder. Had the Bureau failed to get more on the guy? Or had someone withheld vital information?

Something reeked.

If he were a betting man, which he wasn't, he'd bet on the latter. For some reason someone didn't want Ric DiStefano's activities, contacts, whatever, turned into common knowledge — well, common within the Bureau. That raised a multitude of problematic flags.

A few months ago, J.Z. insisted someone in the office had turned. No one could explain how the mob buddies of the money-launderer whose death J.Z. was assigned to investigate had known where to find him no matter what he did to keep his plans secret.

David doodled on a notepad, flipped through the few papers on DiStefano, drank his poison, grew more frustrated with every passing minute. He glugged down his last gulp of lousy coffee, threw down his pencil, grabbed the papers, and rose.

If Eliza was only going to give him these lousy crumbs of info, he was going to have to come up with what he needed on his own. And the first step would be to talk to J.Z., see what he knew that Eliza had either withheld or neglected to include in the file.

He called his friend and fellow agent, just to see if he'd come in that morning. J.Z. invited him down.

"What's up?" J.Z. asked when David walked into the cubicle.

"Did anyone fill you in on what happened last night?"

J.Z. gestured for David to sit, which he did in the beat-up, 1950s vintage, putrid green chair on the opposite side of the desk.

"Dan was here when I came in to work. He mentioned something about a hit-and-run and your grandmother. I couldn't make it add up, but he had to head out, so I didn't ask. Protecting Carlie Papparelli is not the snoozer job he'd expected."

David grinned. "That mob widow struck me as a handful. And when she teamed up with your wife . . . watch out!"

"Don't remind me. I still have nightmares about that day. They could've been killed, and it's only by the grace of God that they're still here."

"Amen, brother."

The two men thought back to the day when J.Z., David and a group of other agents rounded up a handful of mobsters.

Innocent lives had hung in the balance, but they'd carried out the arrests with no one seriously harmed.

"So what's the deal?" J.Z. asked.

David dropped the folder on the paper-littered desk. "Take a look. It won't take you long."

J.Z. opened the manila folder, then let out a long whistle. "How do you get from witnessing a hit-and-run to Ric DiStefano?"

"The victim was his sister."

Another whistle. "Think it might have been a setup?"

"I think if I hadn't deflected the Lexus, she'd be as dead as DiStefano."

"So the question is — What did the 'accident' have to do with her brother?"

David stood and shoved his hands in the back pockets of his khaki pants. "I want to know why she gave me this song and dance about the driver being her dead brother's ghost."

"You're kidding. She didn't really say that, did she?"

"Worse. Not only did she say that, but then she also insisted we didn't need the police, that she was fine. She chalked it all up to exhaustion and stress after her brother's death."

"Is there a rule somewhere that says we

get all the crazy women?"

"Hey, you married one!"

A goofy grin brightened up his friend's normally intense expression. "Yeah, I guess they do have some redeeming qualities, don't they?"

"Maryanne does — lots of them. But Lauren DiStefano, with her bogus ghost story? Give me a break, man. Along with these scraps Eliza tossed at me, it adds up to trouble."

"I wish I could disagree, but I'm on that page. And Eliza assigning you to tail the DiStefano woman? That's the kiss of death."

"You know it. Something's up, and I'm being thrown up against Goliath without a clue."

J.Z. closed the folder and held it out to David. "Have faith. That David did okay by leaning on the Lord. You can't go wrong when you do that, you know."

"In our line of work?" David snorted. "What I can't figure out is the guys who go out there day after day without counting on God's strength. Of course, I'm trusting Him."

"So what's next?"

"The grieving sister has a few questions to answer, don't you think?"

"A few. That's where I'm headed. And

thanks for listening. I wanted to make sure I wasn't being paranoid."

David drove toward Lauren's old-money mansion. He wondered how a guy like Ric DiStefano had wound up with a place like that. Usually, those homes were handed down from one generation to the next. The few that ever came on the market did so because the last generation had failed to reproduce. Had that been the case? Or had DiStefano been mixed up with something more sinister than corporate finance shenanigans?

He parked on the street, right in front of the gorgeous old home. It had probably started out as the gem in the crown of a self-made man, maybe a doctor, lawyer, or even a politician — this was Philadelphia, after all.

He rang the doorbell, then he waited out front for what felt like an eternity. The weather was still rotten, and the icy drizzle's needles stung his face.

Finally, she responded. "Oh!"

"May I come in?" he asked. "I've a couple of questions for you."

She opened the door; her every motion shrieked reluctance.

"Hmm," he murmured. "You could do a guy's ego some harm with that kind of welcome."

Her green eyes flashed. "You aren't welcome, Mr. Latham. But since you came up with an official ID last night, I don't have a choice, do I?"

He shrugged, and stepped inside. The interior matched the exterior of the luxurious mansion. Gleaming wood floors, a sparkling chandelier, rich patterned rugs and a spectacular staircase spoke of old money for construction and new money for upkeep.

He had to find out how illegal the DiStefano money was.

Among other things.

He followed her into a grand living room, what must once have been referred to as a formal parlor. Now it housed a huge cream leather sectional, cushy ottoman, dark wood side tables, and a thick creamy brown area rug under it all.

"Hey, the only thing missing is the widescreen plasma TV."

She sat at the end of the sectional with the loungy part on the end, then shrugged. "Not me, Mr. Latham. All of this belonged to my brother. It's — *was* — his home."

"And now it's yours."

Her sigh held a ton of emotion, but David couldn't identify it all.

"If I can hang on to it."

He took note of her comment, and dropped into the curve of the massive couch. "How about if you give me a few more details. This sounds interesting."

Again, her eyes sparked. "Interesting since it doesn't affect you."

"Oh, but it does," he countered. "You see, you've become my new assignment. Or to put it better, last night's hit-and-run is my business. I need to learn everything about it."

"And that would be because . . . ?"

"Because, Miss DiStefano, I witnessed something I can't explain — something *you* couldn't explain to my satisfaction. So why don't we start at the beginning?"

"What do you want to know?"

For such a soft-spoken woman, Lauren DiStefano could put a sharp bite to her words when she wanted to. "How did you come to live with your brother?"

"He was widowed three years ago and left with a two-year-old son to raise. He didn't want to deal with day care or nannies, and since I'm family and an elementary school teacher, he asked me to help. They're the only relatives I have left so I moved in."

"You gave up your own life to become his housekeeper and babysitter?"

Her eyes did their thing again, but her voice didn't go up, it just took another nip with her words. "If that's the way you see family, then I pity you."

Ouch! "That wasn't exactly what I meant, but —"

"Then what did you mean, Mr. Latham? Your question was quite clear. As an educator, I can understand and carry on a conversation, you know."

He felt his cheeks warm. He had come pretty close to what she'd understood him to say.

"Sorry," he muttered. Then he cleared his throat. "How about we start this again?"

She shrugged.

He didn't blame her.

But he still needed information. "Did you and your brother grow up in this home?"

"Not at all. Ric bought this place when his wife was pregnant."

"So he's had it for about four, maybe five years."

"Just over five now. Mark turned five six weeks ago."

"And you were willing to give up your work to care for your nephew."

"Any day, Mr. Latham. I love Mark as if he were my own."

"I could see that last night, Miss Di-

Stefano. You saved him some serious injuries there. The car just glanced off you, but if it had clipped him, as young as he is, the impact would have done damage."

She shuddered. "That was the worst part of it."

"And how do you feel today?"

"I won't lie to you. I'm sore. Every bit of me aches."

"I was pretty sure you weren't anywhere near as all right as you insisted last night."

"I am all right. I just fell. Feeling sore is one thing, an injury that requires an ambulance and EMTs is another."

"I'll give you that." He felt she'd eased up some, so he went in with another of his questions. "So your brother was quite successful. What kind of work did he do?"

"I don't really know. Something to do with funding and stocks — money matters. I never bothered to ask."

So what did she do? Just suck up the bucks the brother brought in?

He tried again. "I imagine he left you well provided, seeing you'll be raising his son."

"I wish. It appears what he did leave is a mountain of debt. I have to meet with the bank and . . ." She gave a vague wave. "I don't know what you call them. Financial planners? Advisors? Money men, okay?"

"There must be insurance, though."

"Yes, there is, and it's a large sum, but if the debts are as serious as the money men say, then it might not stretch far enough for me to keep the house."

"Then what will you do with your nephew? I mean, I imagine you'll have to get a job again."

"Probably. But Mark is in preschool these days. I hope to find a teaching position at his school or another one nearby."

"That would be nice."

They fell silent for a few moments, and David tried to come up with an effective way to ask what he needed to know. But in the end, he had no luck. He leaned forward and blurted it out.

"So how about you tell me what really happened last night? And don't give me that ghost stuff. Where is your brother? Did he die? Or did he pretend he did? Did he try to run you over? And if he did hit you with that car, why? What does he have against you? Why would your brother want to kill you?"

She gasped.

"No!" the little boy yelled from the parlor door. "My daddy dinn'nt do that to Aunt Lauren. I don't like you. Go 'way! Leave my aunt alone, you ugly . . . um . . . nasty . . .

ah . . . *monster!*"

And right then, David did feel like an ugly monster. Especially when he saw the pain in Lauren DiStefano's tear-filled green eyes.

There were times he really hated his job.

FIVE

Lauren ran to Mark's side. "Hush, honey. It's okay. It's Mr. Latham's job to ask questions, even —" she shot David a poisonous glare "— nasty ones."

By then, David did feel as nasty as dog slobber and even less welcome. He went to defend himself, but Mark proved quicker to the draw.

"You gotta go do time-out in the corner, mister." He pointed toward the back of the room. "That's what Miss Green does at school."

David took the chance to lighten the moment. "So Miss Green spends lots of time standing in the corner. Wow, Mark. She must sure be a greeny-meany."

For a heartbeat, the boy seemed to weigh the sincerity of David's joke. But David saw victory at the quirking of Mark's mouth. Then he burst into a full-blown grin.

"Hey, Aunt Lauren! He made a good funny."

"Yes, Mark. He did."

The look she sent David this time made him feel too many things, too many to identify at once. Yes, she saw the humor in his dopey comment, which made him ridiculously proud of himself. But she didn't trust him any more than she would an angry rattler, which for some reason made him want to prove himself — to the subject of an investigation. Go figure.

And she hadn't forgiven his blunt and hurtful questions. Questions he still needed answered.

He sighed. He couldn't very well badger her with the boy in the room. He'd lost his opportunity, and he'd have to bide his time. Because the opportunity would arise again. He'd make sure of it.

He rose. "I see I've overstayed my welcome."

"Hey!" Mark cried. "Aren't you gonna stand in the corner?"

The boy's frown broadcast what he thought of David shirking punishment.

"Ah . . . sure," he backpedaled. "I'll check out the corner of my office. And I will think about all those nasty questions I asked."

Two pairs of green eyes studied him, very

different messages in them.

"You gonna ask 'em again?" The boy's wisdom caught David by surprise.

Lauren smiled, but it wasn't a happy smile. "Oh, I'm sure he won't, Mark. He's going to come up with new, nastier ones, I'm afraid."

The boy planted his fists on his slim hips. "You're gonna spend lots a time in time-out then, mister. You better like your corner a whole bunch."

David's cheeks tingled again. "From the mouths of babes . . ."

"Let me show you out, Mr. Latham." Lauren's otherwise polite voice had that nip back again. "Mark and I are busy this afternoon, and we must get ready."

The boy's eyes grew big and round. "We are?"

"Of course, we are." A touch of pink brightened her creamy cheeks. "We're going to the library."

"Sudden need for a good book, huh?"

Her chin tipped up, and she strode to the front door. "Always. Reading is an absolute necessity, Mr. Latham. You'd be surprised by how many take the ability to read for granted and don't even make use of it."

A blast of frigid air rushed in the open doorway — it matched the temperature of her voice as she added, "It's by far the best road to true wisdom."

"Hmm . . . and here I thought that road ran through God's Word."

"And how does one access the Father's Word, Mr. Latham?"

"Touché!" He stepped past her and into the cold. "But there is one thing you really, really have to do — or stop doing."

He didn't let her ask. "It's that Mr. Latham thing, okay? I keep looking over my shoulder to see if my dad's standing somewhere behind me. My name's David, okay?"

She shrugged. "I'm hoping not to have to use either one again."

"Ouch!" He struck a theatrical pose with a hand over his heart. "You wound me so, Miss DiStefano. And me, a poor wandering soldier on a mission."

Her snort caught him off guard. "Someone's called you charming much too often, but you won't charm me. I've seen you at work."

"Which is where I need to be," he conceded. "Have a good afternoon at the library. See ya, Mark!"

The little boy turned to his aunt. When she nodded, he faced David. "Bye, Mr. Latham."

David loped down the front steps, careful

to avoid globs of heavy slush here and there. He knew trouble when he saw it; he could lose his heart to the little fellow.

Once in his car, he looked back at the mansion, and caught the curtain's movement in the front window. He hadn't seen her, but he didn't need to. He knew Lauren had watched him get into his car.

Something about that woman intrigued him.

And it had nothing to do with her brother. Or her nephew. Not even his job.

David's gut told him he was in trouble — big trouble.

He started to pray.

After she told David she and Mark were library-bound, Lauren couldn't not go. Although she came up with the idea as a way to get the man out of the house, she often did take Mark to Story Hour in the children's section. It was an every-afternoon event at their small local branch, so her nephew didn't need much of an explanation.

While the children were busy, Lauren usually satisfied her hunger for fresh reading material. She read all the time — even the jokes and stories on the back of a cereal box made do in a pinch. But that day Lauren just wandered the racks. She didn't bother to search for anything. She couldn't focus on her surroundings.

What had really happened on that dark, slushy street? In that moment when the car hurtled toward her, she saw a face she knew almost as well as her own. But it couldn't have been Ric. And now she had to wonder if stress really had taken over her common sense, as she'd told David.

Her brother's death had come as a complete shock. True, Ric had been a lot older, but he'd also been in her world her entire life. As a child, she'd always seen him as the hero brother any little girl could want. He'd spoiled her, treated her like a princess. But then he'd finished high school, headed to college, and she'd been left behind.

She hardly ever saw him after that. Sure, she was in his wedding, she visited when Mark was born, but other than that and the occasional holiday, as years went by, theirs became a card-here-and-there relationship. That's why, after her parents' deaths, and then that of her sister-in-law, when Ric called and asked if she'd be willing to devote herself to little Mark, she hadn't hesitated.

"Aunt Lauren, Aunt Lauren!"

She turned, saw him and the other Story Hour kids burst from the room like a circus of fleas run amok.

"Ready?" she asked.

"Uh-huh."

On the way home, Lauren bought a copy of the evening paper. She did have to start that job hunt. The words of the headmistress at her former school lingered in the back of her mind. "You'll always have a position here, Lauren. We want you back."

But to get to that school she had to drive all the way across town. She didn't think it would be in Mark's best interest to uproot him from the preschool he liked so much just because she had to commute to work. She hoped to find something closer to home.

If she managed to hang on to the home.

But gloom and doom wouldn't get her anywhere, so she turned to the Lord in prayer. She asked for wisdom, for strength, for guidance. She couldn't see how she was going to pull it all off, but she had faith the Father would see her through.

At home, she made a simple meal of grilled chicken, salad and savory seasoned rice. She watched a children's video with Mark, listened to his prayers, and then tucked him into bed. From the doorway, she watched him doze off, a wealth of maternal love in her heart.

She couldn't love him more if he were her own.

Lauren frowned. She'd told David those very words, or some very much like those, not so long ago. And just that fast, once again, thoughts of her troubles returned. But the events of the last month had left her tired, drained, exhausted. And then that car . . .

She pushed the concerns of the day to one side, changed into a nightgown, washed her face, brushed her teeth and crawled under her blankets, Bible in hand.

After a good, long while with the Lord, she set the Holy Book on her nightstand, and turned off the light.

But later on, much later, she didn't know quite how long, a child's cry pierced her sleep. Lauren sat up with a start, heart racing, head whirling, temples pounding.

Mark!

"It's okay, honey!" She grabbed her comfy old chenille bathrobe and ran from the room. "I'm coming."

His cries didn't ease, but rather intensified as she approached his open door. She always left it ajar, just in case he needed her — as he did right then.

By the soft glow of his robot night-light, Lauren saw him sitting in the middle of a puddle of blankets. His little boy's eyes looked enormous in his pale face, and tears shone on his cheeks. Mark leaped right up into her open arms.

"What's wrong?" she asked. "Did you have a bad dream. . . ."

Her words trailed off when she felt the wetness soak through where his legs wrapped around her waist. *Uh-oh!*

Mark hadn't wet the bed in years. "Oh, sweetheart . . . let's get you cleaned up."

She went to put him down, but his arms tightened in a stranglehold around her neck and he burrowed deeper into her embrace.

"No!" he screamed, his warm, sturdy body shaking. "The lights . . . they're coming, Aunt Lauren! They're coming. . . ."

Sobs overtook him again, and nothing could have budged his hold on her. Not that she really wanted to let go of him, but the night was cold, and by now, they both were soaked. Still, something far worse than wet nightclothes and linens had gone wrong here. And it didn't take a psychiatrist to figure it out.

"Mark, honey. The lights — the car — didn't hurt us. Mr. Latham's car blocked the other one, and it only gave me a little bump. But I'm all right, and you didn't get hurt one bit. It's okay. We're home, and no one's going to hurt us."

She hoped.

He shook his head — hard. "No! No-no-no-no-no-no-no!"

Tears flew from his eyes, cheeks, and struck her. His misery was so deep, his fear so intense that her own eyes welled up in sympathy. She perched on the edge of the bed, aware of the soaked middle.

"It's okay," she murmured yet again, her voice little more than a croon. "I'm here, and I won't let the car hit you. You know Aunt Lauren always takes care of you, right?"

Her gentle rocking motion must have helped. His muscles no longer felt like short steel ropes in her arms, and his sobs didn't sound as though ripped right from his soul. But he didn't answer her. Evidently, he still couldn't.

She began to sing. "Jesus loves me, this I know . . ."

Lauren sang her entire repertoire of children's tunes, praise and worship songs, and even a hymn or ten, before Mark's tears ran dry. Finally, even though he'd stopped crying, she knew he hadn't fallen back asleep. His eyes glowed their clear green in the dark of the quiet room.

"Think you might want some clean pj's

now, kiddo?"

His fingers fisted in her robe.

"I'm not going anywhere," she said, a hint of humor in her voice. "At least, I'm not going anywhere without you — you got that?"

His lips took on a slight upward curve. "Promise?"

"Absotively, posilutely, babe. You and me . . . we're a team."

He giggled. "You got it wrong again, Aunt Lauren. It's abos-No, no! Not abos. Ab-*so*little, pos . . . posilately!"

"So, tell me, Mark. Are you ready for those clean jammies now?"

Even by the dim glow of the night-light, she saw his cheeks turn red. He lowered his gaze, and whispered, "I'm sorry. I dinn'nt mean to . . . to —"

"I know, honey. It was an accident, and I bet it happened during that bad dream. Right?"

He nodded.

"So . . . when an accident happens, we clean up the mess, fix whatever's broken, and ask God to help us go on. What do you think?"

"Mmm-hmm." He turned his face into her chest, rubbed his nose against her robe and nodded. "Smells good, Aunt Lauren."

She chuckled. "Tell you what, pal. Let's get some water in the tub, clean you up and put you into pajamas that smell exactly like my robe."

"It's that soften stuff, isn't it?"

"Fabric softener. A true modern marvel, my friend."

Lauren eased him off her lap, turned on the bedside lamp, and then rummaged through his dresser for clean clothes. She stripped the bed, redid it with fabric-softener-scented sheets, and then piled the mess outside his bedroom door.

"Here we go, into the deep blue yonder . . ." she warbled.

Holding hands, they marched into the adjoining red-and-white bathroom. She ran the water, Mark stripped, hopped into the tub and she ran the pajamas and linens down to the laundry room. As she went through the kitchen, she thought she heard a scratch at the back door.

Ooooh, that cat!

"Go away, Adolf! I have no fish bones for you."

She felt sorry for the neighbors' ratty-looking tomcat. The Scharffenbergers let the poor animal run wild most of the time, and Philly's winters were notoriously cold and mean. Still, the critter had outstayed his never-warm welcome in her yard. She'd had to rig up an Adolf-proof system for trash can storage, otherwise, the half-eared thing would knock them over and strew garbage all down the drive.

Still, as much of a trial as he was, Lauren couldn't make herself rat on the neighbors. She figured the ugly cat's lot would worsen at the pound. No normal child would beg a mother to take the big, fat, mean-as-a-snake thing home. So she never failed to bungee-cord the trash cans shut and set the brakes on the wheeled, aluminum-rail-sided cart where she kept them.

Evidently, her yell sent her nocturnal visitor elsewhere. By the time she dumped the stinky bedclothes into the washer, poured a capful of detergent and one of softener into the appropriate dispensers, all she could hear was Mark's happy splashing directly overhead.

She closed the washer, turned the knob to the right setting and started the cycle. One of the songs she'd sung to Mark just a while earlier came back to her, and she hummed a few bars on the way back to the front of the house.

Then she heard it again.

The scratching sound.

At the front door.

Her heartbeat sped up. Her breath caught in her throat. The fear she'd felt as the car rushed at her returned. Her muscles felt frozen, but she knew she had to act.

Mark!

"Lord Jesus," she whispered on the first step up, "guide me, protect Mark, and keep me safe so I can care for him. . . ."

Screetch! Scratch-scrape-scrape, screeeee-eetch!

Whoever was out there meant to pick that lock.

Lauren gave up on stealth and ran the rest of the way up to her room. She picked up the phone, but all she heard when she put the receiver to her ear was deafening silence.

He'd cut the line.

She ran for her purse. "Thank you, Father, for cell phones!"

On the way to the bathroom, she hit 911. In bursts of whispers, she relayed her plight to the dispatcher. The kind woman assured her she'd sent for help, then kept her on the line, her warm voice a comfort within the swirl of danger around her.

Lauren knew better than to expect a siren; the dispatcher had told her the officers wouldn't want to alert the intruder.

Still, she kept listening for . . . something, she didn't know what, but a signal that would tell her she and Mark were safe, that help had arrived.

Mark was still in the water, splashing his rubber toys in complete oblivion — just the way Lauren wanted it. The last thing the child needed, right on the heels of that terrible nightmare, was another fright. And an intruder in the wee hours of the night was nothing but frightening.

Then pandemonium broke out.

A car drove by at normal speed.

At the front door, a man shouted a curse.

Blazing lights strobed into the house despite the curtains on the windows. She heard scrambling, more voices, more cars. Brakes squealed, doors slammed shut.

"Stop!" someone hollered.

Another car sped up, this one's tires crunching ice and snow and finally shrieking against the pavement. Others followed, and did the same. A heartbeat later, someone pounded on her front door.

"Open up!" a familiar voice shouted.

Lauren looked at Mark, whose eyes were again wide-open, round, frightened. His mouth formed an O, and his naked limbs shook with fear.

The pounding downstairs never let up.

He yelled again. "Lauren! Let me in! It's David — David Latham."

"The monster," Mark sobbed. "No, Aunt Lauren! Don't let him in. He's gonna . . . he's gonna eat us up!"

And although she knew Monster David didn't have a cannibalistic bent, Lauren hesitated.

How could she let that man inside her house again? How could she subject Mark to another trauma? The child had suffered too much already.

But someone had tried to break into her house. She'd heard them at the back and front doors, she'd heard the curse when the cops drove up, heard the running footsteps when they gave pursuit.

And David was a Federal Agent.

Even though he didn't seem to believe her, she didn't think he would hurt them, while the intruder wouldn't have any such qualms.

She took a deep breath. "It's okay, Marky. Everything's going to be okay."

The bright red-green-and-purple-striped bath sheet she used to wrap her nephew felt wrong in their current situation. It belonged to happy summer days, not to a horrifying winter night.

Still, she held the boy close to her heart and ran down the stairs. David's pounding grew louder the closer she came. At this rate, she wouldn't have much of a door left by the time she let him in.

She ran.

Mark shook.

Her fingers trembled on the doorknob. She finally got everything to work, threw open the door and glared at the enraged man on her front step. Before he could get a word out, she spoke.

"You'd better have your checkbook ready to pay for a new door, Agent Latham. It was an irreplaceable antique."

He scowled. "Forget the door, lady. It's fine. It's your irreplaceable lives I care about. You and the boy could've been killed!"

Lauren's knees shook then gave way.

On the way down, her only thought was of Mark. The child whose weight left her arms as she slid into a midnight-black hole.

Six

Lauren woke up in the hospital. She could identify her surroundings before she opened her eyes. The astringent smell of rubbing alcohol and disinfectant stung her nostrils, and the eerie chill of IV fluids flowing into her hand was unmistakable. Her appendectomy two years ago had left her with indelible memories, few of them good.

As she grew more alert, she took note of the angle at which her bed was propped and the voices above her. Then she pried open one eye. The disgusting pea-green of the wall she saw confirmed her surroundings.

Seconds later, Lauren recognized one of the voices — hers. She'd been speaking, but she had no idea what she'd said. And the people she'd been talking to? She had no idea who they were, either. Confusion reigned supreme.

"Excuse me," she managed to croak out.

At least this time she knew what she'd said.

A freckled female face materialized in her line of sight. "Hey, Shakespeare! You done emoting?" she asked, a twinkle in her gray eyes.

Lauren wrinkled her nose. "Shakespeare?"

The woman fiddled with the IV valve and nodded. Her deep auburn ponytail swept down over one shoulder. "A real ragbag of bits and pieces. My favorite?" Her grin turned mischievous. "Macbeth's witches!"

"At least I offer the best of the best." Lauren turned to look at the others in the room.

Big mistake.

Pain shot up the back of her head to the crown and down into her forehead. The gross pea-green of the walls spun around the white of the privacy curtain, crashed into the blue of the redhead's top, added the black of a man's clothes to the mix, and tossed in the silver sparkle of the bedrails and IV pole.

The smell of antiseptic combined with that of something not as acceptable and the rare brew made her stomach lurch. She gritted her teeth so as not to throw up.

"Look!" a man said. "She's smiling. She must be feeling better."

The redhead rolled her eyes. "Trust me.

That's no smile. She's in a world of pain right now, and she's probably trying not to scream."

A school-bus-yellow mountain approached the bed. Lauren's stomach roiled. Her face grew cold then the rest of her body followed that icy trend. The nausea intensified, and she moaned.

"Watch out, Davey!" the sunny Mt. Rushmore warned. "She's about to vomit!"

"Really?" Mark asked, excitement in his voice. "Aunt Lauren's gonna barf? Cool!"

Noooooo! she wanted to yell, but Lauren was afraid if she quit biting down long enough to speak, she really would throw up. So instead she did the single worse thing she could've done: she shook her head.

Alice's fall through the looking glass couldn't have been any more disconcerting than the changes Lauren's world underwent. The lights went out; they came back on but changed colors just as fast — red, purple, green, blue; voices rose then fell silent. Through it all, only one thing stayed steady: the pain in her head.

Another heartfelt moan slipped out past her lips.

The redhead wasn't happy. "Hey! If you guys can't keep quiet on your own, then I'm going to have to use my surgical tape on you. This woman needs peace and quiet. She's got herself a scrambled brain, and you aren't helping."

A concussion? How had that happened? Had someone hit her on the head? Who would have done that?

Lauren remembered opening the door to David Latham. Then pitch black had smothered her. She had to know how she'd landed in the hospital, so she forced herself to take calm, even breaths and kept her head very, very still. Little by little the nausea subsided.

"Why am I here?" she asked, glad her voice didn't crack. "What happened?"

"You fell, Aunt Lauren. Right by the door. And you smacked your head on the floor. You should'a seen all the blood, too. What a mess!"

That didn't surprise her; the granite floor was far harder than her poor head. She remembered holding the boy close right before everything went black. "Are you all right, Marky?"

"Aw, Aunt Lauren. I told you not to call me that."

She smiled and opened her eyes. "Just checking. Now I know you're fine."

"Well!" Mt. Rushmore said. "Let me tell you something, honey. He's not going to stop that nonsense with the nicknames —

not now, not ever. No matter how old he gets. I should know."

Just beyond one solid yellow shoulder, Lauren spotted David Latham, dressed in all black. He held her nephew in his arms.

"Come on, Gram," the FBI agent cajoled. "Give her a break. She doesn't need your nuttiness right now."

That was David's grandmother? Lauren took a better look at the woman. While no one would call her beautiful, she had what in earlier times was known as a handsome face. Straight dark brows flew out over brown eyes that, unless she was much mistaken, missed nothing. Short white hair spiked in a youthful, sassy style that somehow fit despite her age. Surprisingly few lines marked a smooth golden complexion, and scarlet lipstick drew attention to a brilliant smile.

A smile directed at her. "How're you feeling?"

For a moment, Lauren considered the polite "Fine." But something about those perceptive brown eyes told her the truth would do far better. "Lousy."

David's grandmother laughed. "I like her, Davey. Is this the one from the car the other night?"

"That was just night before last, Gram,

and yes, this is Lauren DiStefano."

The older woman faced Lauren again. "He's got no manners, this boy of mine. Hi, Lauren DiStefano. I'm pleased to meet you. I'm Dorothea Latham, but everyone calls me Grandma Dottie. Please do."

Lauren didn't know quite what to make of the woman or her offer, so she simply said, "Thanks."

Grandma Dottie studied her a little longer then smiled again. "We're going to get along just fine." She placed a hand on Lauren's shoulder. "Now, honey. I know this is going to be tough for you, but I want you to understand. I'm only trying to help you out here."

Lauren tensed. "What . . . how are you trying to help? I don't understand."

"I'm sorry." The spikes wobbled as Grandma Dottie shook her head. "I didn't do that very well, now, did I? You're going to have to stay strapped to that contraption —" she pointed to the IV pole "— at least overnight. And from what Davey tells me, that little fellow there is all alone but for you."

Alarm made Lauren try to sit. The pain made her fall back against the pillow. She shut her eyes tight and pursed her lips. "He is."

The hand on her shoulder tightened a fraction. "It's okay, dear. I know that upset you. I told Davey it would, but unless you want Children's Services to come into the picture, we're going to have to work with what we have."

"And that would be you," Lauren murmured.

"That would be me."

"And me," David offered. "Mark and I get along great, don't we, pal?"

" 'S right, Monster Man."

Lauren didn't know whether to laugh or cry. "Mark! That's not a very nice thing to say —"

"But that's what he told me to call him, Aunt Lauren. I dinn'nt do something wrong, did I?"

She met David's gaze. He wanted her to go along with him, and she realized it was in Mark's best interest if she did. The boy really was all alone but for her. At least he'd come to accept David, a supposedly trustworthy FBI agent, and David had a grandmother in the wings willing to help out.

But could she really trust them with Mark? Did she even have a choice? She couldn't sit up, much less take her nephew and run. Besides, there was something very solid, very sincere about Grandma Dottie.

She sighed. "No, Marky. You didn't do anything wrong."

"There!" Grandma Dottie exclaimed. "Now that we have that all straightened out, why don't I take Mark down to the self-serve machines and get him something good to drink?"

The brown eyes telegraphed a clear message to Lauren. She nodded. "Sounds great. I wish I could come with you, but enjoy every last drop for me, kiddo."

A pang of anxiety shot through her as the boy ran out of the room at Grandma Dottie's side. *Father God, please don't let this be the last time I see him. Don't let me fail with him.*

"Thanks," David said at her side. "I know it must be tough to let him go, but I couldn't think of anything else to do here. I couldn't leave him alone, and your house is being scoured with a fine-tooth comb for clues of any kind. We couldn't go back there. Plus Gram's great with kids — I can vouch for that."

"She seems great, period."

He shrugged. "She is. I'm surprised you figured that out so quick, especially with the bump you got to the head. How do you feel, by the way?"

"I'm usually quite good at pegging people,

Mr. Latham. I doubt a minor injury would change that. I also suspect you've earned a concussion or two in your line of work, so I'm sure you know how awful I feel."

"I'm sorry about that. I had to make a choice. You were going down, and you had Mark all wrapped up in that crazy towel. The end of the thing got tangled up with your legs, and I couldn't grab both of you."

"I'm glad you grabbed Mark."

"I figured you'd say that, but I still don't feel right about it. I wish I could have caught you, too."

"Please don't worry about it. I'll be fine. I'm sure they'll let me leave soon. You know how hospitals are. They ship you out no sooner than they get you in."

"Not hardly," the redhead said. "You're not going anywhere for at least twenty-four hours. We gotta keep an eye on you. Can't have you dropping again and popping our excellent embroidery wide open, you know."

What a character! "But I have a child to look after —"

"He looked pretty chipper to me," she countered as she adjusted a knob on a machine with green squiggles against a black background. "Unlike you."

David chuckled. "You got that right. For a minute there, I thought you were going to do as Gram said."

"I don't vomit easily, Mr. Latham."

He gave her a long look. "You keep yourself on a tight leash, don't you?"

"I'm sure I don't know what you mean by that. Unless you're speaking of self-control."

"What else would I mean? And you do it so well."

"I like to think of myself as a civilized woman."

"You mean, unlike the rest of us mortals?"

"No! I'm not at all like that."

This time, his gaze asked questions she couldn't decipher, wasn't even sure she wanted to, never mind answer.

"What are you really like, Lauren DiStefano? Who are you?"

"Who am I?" She glared. "*That* is a terrible question. I'm me. That's all. Just me."

"And who exactly is that?" He quirked up the corner of his lips in a strange, humorless smile. "You'd better know the answer to that question, because we're going to discuss it at great length."

After that outrageous statement, he touched his forehead with two fingers, turned and left her room. Lauren felt the urge to run, go after Grandma Dottie, grab Mark, make her escape.

But she didn't know what she had to escape.

The intruder had gone.

He hadn't hurt her or Mark.

The car was also gone. It hadn't done much harm.

But David? Yes, he'd left. But not for long. He would return.

And Lauren didn't know if she'd be ready to see him again.

Was he the one she had to flee?

Confusion reigned supreme . . . hadn't she said that before?

"Lord? What's happening to me? Please help. I need to be well, strong. I need to look out for Mark."

But no matter how she prayed, Lauren couldn't shake the feeling that Mark wasn't the one in David Latham's sights. He was after her.

The question was why?

As it turned out, Colleen, Lauren's red-haired nurse, was right. The doctor had refused to let her leave the hospital for twenty-four hours. During that frustrating time, though, Lauren got to know Grandma Dottie a little better.

The woman knew how much Lauren needed to see her nephew, and she'd had him at her bedside every chance she could. The kindness David's grandmother offered with such generosity and her fabulous way with Mark stole Lauren's heart.

When it came time for her to leave, it was Grandma Dottie who came to pick her up. An orderly drove her mandatory wheelchair down to the discharge door. The two of them lost the ability to speak when the purple Hummer drove up.

"Isn't she pretty?" Grandma Dottie said, patting the vehicle's hood. "I traded in my wimpy car for this beauty. She can really roar."

Lauren blinked hard a couple of times, but the sight of the elderly woman praising the erstwhile military vehicle — painted purple, no less — didn't change.

"*You* drive that?"

"You betcha!" Grandma Dottie said. "And Mark loves it, too."

What little boy wouldn't? "I'm sure."

"Come on! Let's get this show on the road," David's grandmother said. "We're going to take a spin. Tell me how you like her, okay?"

Lauren chuckled. "Okay. If you're sure you won't mind whatever I say."

The orderly and Grandma Dottie helped Lauren up into the mammoth vehicle. The young man closed the door, and Lauren's eccentric chauffeur ran around to the driver's side.

"Buckle up!" Dorothea Latham sang out.

They absolutely did roar.

When they pulled up in front of the DiStefano home, Lauren didn't quite know what to say. She opted for a noncommittal, "Interesting."

Grandma Dottie winked. "I'll get you yet."

Lauren wouldn't put it past the older woman. "But I can't begin to afford a beast like this, so it won't matter."

"You can borrow mine any time you want," Grandma Dottie said as she took Mark out of the booster seat. "I love to share."

They went inside, put the boy down to continue his nap, and Lauren decided she'd much rather camp out on the front parlor sofa than lie in bed upstairs. Grandma Dottie wouldn't let her even walk to the kitchen. She insisted on bringing a tray full of an impressive assortment of treats for their lunch.

The two women sipped asparagus soup, crunched vegetables with spinach dip, savored quarter-cut ham, egg salad, tuna, and roast beef sandwiches, and for dessert, cloud-light pumpkin custards hit the spot.

Lauren patted her mouth with her napkin. "I'm going to burst."

"Pshaw!" Grandma Dottie took the tray littered with the remains of their meal and headed for the door. "You're wasting away, dear. We have to put meat on your bones. And I won't take no for an answer."

Lauren's mother had died when she was nineteen and in college. Since then, she hadn't been pampered and spoiled like this. Although she felt guilty letting an elderly woman serve her, there was little she could do about it. Her body betrayed her with its ongoing weakness, and Grandma Dottie defeated her with her incredible strength of character. Lauren drifted off to sleep in no time.

The doorbell woke her up. Outside, dusk had arrived. The streetlight from the corner cast the tree by the large window into long shadows across the dark parlor. Lauren tried to stand, but found herself tucked into a blanket.

"Don't get up," Grandma Dottie called out. "I'll get the door."

Lauren smiled. She could get used to this, especially since her head still hurt when she moved it more quickly than she should. The bandage itched, and she didn't appreciate the hunk of hair they'd shaved off at the hospital.

She heard Grandma Dottie speak. A male voice she didn't recognize responded. They talked back and forth, and then the door closed with a firm thud.

David's grandmother walked back into the parlor, a puzzled expression on her face. "That was the strangest thing."

"What? What's wrong?"

"I'm not sure anything's wrong. That man, though, is an odd one, I'll give you that."

"Who was he?"

"Beats me. Says his name's not important, and he wants the bird."

"The bird?"

"That's what he said. The bird. And he asked for it over and over and over again."

"That is strange. I don't have a bird. He must have come to the wrong house."

"That's what I thought, too, but then he showed me a scrap of paper with the address. He had that right."

Lauren shook her head. "The bird . . ."

"The bird."

"Did he say anything else? Anything at all?"

"Well, he did say someone named Rick had told him to come get the bird."

Lauren went cold. "You're sure he said . . . Ric?"

Grandma Dottie nodded. "Do you know a Rick?"

Lauren drew a deep breath. "My brother's name was Ric. But he died almost a month ago."

"Oh, dear. Maybe they'd come to some agreement about this bird before your brother died, but this fellow only now got around to coming for it."

All of a sudden, the headlights rushed straight at Lauren again. Fear gripped her. Terror froze her. She moaned.

"Lauren!" Grandma Dottie cried. "Lauren, are you all right? What's wrong? Oh, Father, help us!"

The moments trickled by.

Lauren fought for her sanity, but it seemed to have abandoned her the day her brother died. Everything had changed. Nothing was the same.

First that crazy Boris . . . whatever. And now, this other stranger showed up looking for Ric . . . or for Ric's bird. A bird she never knew he had.

As if in a trance, she watched Grandma Dottie dial a number on a cell phone. She spoke in a quiet voice, but she seemed clear on what she wanted to say . . . unlike Lauren, who had no idea what to say, what to do, what was real, what was not.

When the older woman ended her conversation, Lauren forced herself to get a grip. "I'm okay," she said.

"Sure thing. Just like I'm wearing Kate Moss's favorite outfit tonight."

Lauren couldn't avoid the chuckle. "Sorry about that."

"That's just what I wanted to see. A smile."

She shrugged. "You have to admit, things have been pretty strange in my life lately."

"More than strange, I'd say."

"Speaking of things said, did our visitor say anything else?"

Grandma Dottie waved her hand. "Sure. He said he'd be back tomorrow for his bird. He suggested you look for it 'real good.' "

Lauren took a deep breath. "It must have been Ric's, but I don't think he ever kept whatever it might be in the house. I've never seen a bird in the three years I've lived here. I don't know if we can find it before the man returns."

"We nothing," David said from the door.

Lauren looked up in surprise. "Where'd you come from?"

"Outside. Don't forget. You're my assignment."

"So you're camping on my front door?"

"If you say so." He grinned. "I'd rather think I'm living out of my car."

Lauren didn't know whether she liked knowing he was that close or if it scared her even more. "Did you see our visitor?"

"Couldn't miss him."

"Do you know him?"

"He came to see you, not me."

Grandma Dottie cleared her throat. "I'm the one who opened the door. I insisted Lauren sleep after lunch, and I sure didn't know him."

"Know what he wanted?" David asked.

"The bird —"

"Some bird —"

He frowned. "You have a bird?"

"Not me," Lauren answered. "Ric. Or at least that's what the man told your grandmother. And he insists we find it. He's coming back for the stupid thing tomorrow."

David narrowed his eyes. "Then we'll look for a bird. Tomorrow. Tonight you have to rest."

"But he's coming back tomorrow —"

"We'll look in the morning. And I'll answer the door when he comes."

Lauren shivered. Going by David's hard stare, the man who wanted the bird was going to get more than he'd asked for. He was getting a suspicious, determined, tough-as-nails FBI agent, and if he was lucky, a bird.

She was glad she wasn't the man.

She doubted things would go well for him.

Not if David had anything to do with it. And he did.

SEVEN

The next morning spun by more like a part of Alice's famous adventures in Wonderland than anything remotely related to Lauren's life. David was everywhere. And he made his presence known.

Even his grandmother, who clearly doted on him, soon had enough of his orders.

"That's it!" she cried. "David Andrew Latham, I've had about all I can take of this I'm-a-whoop-de-do-FBI-agent business. Neither Lauren nor I are incompetent, and we're in no way, shape or form here for you to boss around, buddy boy. So if you want to help search this massive museum, then you're going to have to mind your p's and q's."

Lauren bit back her laughter.

David clenched his jaw then eased his shoulders and winked. "I've always wondered what that p's and q's business means, Gram. Wanna let me in on the secret?"

Grandma Dottie crossed her arms and glared. "You know perfectly well what it means, so you'd better dig for some of those manners you were taught. Put them to good use, and remember the please and thank-yous — the p's and q's you conveniently forget."

"Woo-hoo!" Mark crowed. "Monster Man's going back in the corner, Aunt Lauren. 'S what happens when you forget your manners, you know."

Monster Man laughed. "Only if you come hang out in that boring corner with me, Mark the Man."

"No way! I dinn'nt forget nothing. . . ."

And they took off, Mark on David's heels. Once again, as she watched her nephew follow his new hero, Lauren experienced that surreal feeling, that sense of lost control, that had overtaken her life since Ric's death. She couldn't stomach the feeling any longer. The time had come to change things.

And she'd start by finding that stupid bird.

She hadn't been up on the third floor in the last three plus weeks. But now, with that strange man's looming return, she had to overcome her natural reluctance and go search through her brother's belongings for the bird — whatever shape or form it might take.

"At least he's good for something — babysitting," Grandma Dottie said. "Lauren, dear, I'm on my way back down to the basement. Beats me how someone can pack so much stuff into one house when they only lived in it for five years."

"You'd have to have known Ric." Lauren laughed. "He was the worst pack rat! He never threw anything out, so the basement is stuffed. His rooms on the third floor can't be much better, so that's where I'll start. I only wish I knew what we were looking for. Good luck."

"Back atcha!"

With a prayer for courage, Lauren climbed the two flights of stairs to the floor Ric took as his own after his wife's death. He'd told Lauren not to worry about it, that he knew how messy he was, that he'd clean up after himself. In the three years since she moved in, she'd only maintained the bathroom and kept the linen closet there supplied with clean sheets and towels.

Now she had to breach his privacy.

She opened the bedroom door and stepped inside. The drapes were drawn, just as he must have left them. The shrouded window cast a sense of gloom over everything. With a deep breath, she squared her shoulders, marched right over, leaned across a couple of boxes on the floor, tugged aside the heavy antique satin draperies, and welcomed the fresh new day.

Pale winter sunlight poured in. "That's better," she murmured then turned around and gave the room a good look.

Never in a million years could she have imagined what she saw. Boxes upon boxes rose from the floor to almost ceiling height. They hid every wall, and at the foot of the double bed, three additional boxes replaced a more typical bench or chest.

"What in the world . . . ?"

But no one answered her question; no one could. And while the room was anything but messy, the boxes posed a mystery she felt inadequate to solve. What had Ric packed and stacked so methodically? Why had he done it? And did one of the boxes hide a bird? What kind of bird was it? Was it stuffed? Carved? Painted?

"Well, I certainly won't find out until I open them, will I, Lord?"

With a sigh, she plopped down at the foot of the bed and tore the packing tape off the nearest box. That one had papers; file folders filled with pages full of the same kind of numbers, facts, figures and sums. Clearly business materials.

Lauren moved on to the next box. That

one held more of the same. As did the last one at its side and the three others under the window. If she wanted to make any headway now, she'd have to tackle the stacks.

Fortunately, the boxes she'd checked were on the small side and not too heavy. She pushed a couple over to the first wall, piled one on the other, and then clambered up.

Now what?

She could think of no good reason to dismantle Ric's warehouse-in-a-bedroom. How would she ever put it all back together again if she did? What could she do to check out the contents of the boxes?

She had an idea, and ran down to the kitchen. In her catchall drawer, among the rubber bands, twisty ties, odd screws, broken pencils, paper scraps and dried-up pens, she kept a utility knife. She grabbed it then trotted back up the stairs, pausing to catch her breath on the second-floor landing. She really had to stop the up-and-down treks; her head had started to pound again.

Methodically, she cut out small squares from the side of every box. In no time, she'd checked them all. None contained anything that by any stretch of the imagination resembled a bird — all were full of folders stuffed with papers full of the same kind of numbers, facts, figures and sums.

She moved on to the walk-in closet. Suits in a complete masculine range of colors lined one side. Dress shirts and sport shirts hung from a top rack on the opposite side, and below the shirts, clip hangers held slacks of many colors. Partway down each wall, a drawer stack rose from floor to ceiling, and a quick tug showed her the contents of each: socks, underwear, polo shirts, sweaters, handkerchiefs, etc. His handcrafted shoes spread out under all the clothes, shiny and neat.

Why would Ric have described himself as messy? From the looks of the room, he'd been a complete neat freak.

The back wall held a collection of huge garment bags. Lauren unzipped one at random. A spill of sparkly, multi-colored sequins burst from within the somber black plastic to catch the light of the overhead fixture. The extravagant fabric puddled to the floor, dragged down by the weight of the tens of thousands of sequins and beads.

She shook her head. "His Mummers' stuff."

Ric had been a member of a New Year's Eve Mummers' and Shooters' Brigade, one of the "fancies." All Lauren knew about the group was that they gathered on a regular basis during the year for the sole purpose of creating the lavish costumes the men would wear for Philly's traditional New Year's Day parade. Over the years, the spectacle had become famous, and many traveled to the City of Brotherly Love to watch the brigades march and play their music come rain, shine or snow.

Lauren knelt to pick up the costume, one Ric had worn two years ago. Just then, she heard Mark run up the stairs.

"You up here, Aunt Lauren? We're hungry. Grandma Dottie says lunch is ready. You wanna come eat —"

He stopped at the door and stared. "Daddy's mummy stuff."

The longing on her nephew's face tugged at Lauren's heart. "Come here, honey."

Mark came, tears in his eyes. "I miss my daddy. . . ."

His tears turned into sobs. She held him close. "I know you do, Mark. I miss him, too."

And she did. Even though she hadn't seen Ric much, not even during the last three years when they'd lived in the same house. Still, Lauren had always known her brother to be . . . there, where she could reach him if she needed him. But now he wasn't.

Ric had been eccentric, his love for the

105

pageantry of the Mummers' tradition one of his more unusual peculiarities. But she'd always felt his love, and no one could have doubted his feelings for his son.

For that reason, she still couldn't come to grips with the accident, the hit-and-run, much less the face she'd seen behind the windshield. Ric wouldn't have tried to kill her. Or Mark. Not the Ric she'd known all her life.

Would he?

A disturbing question occurred to her. How well had she really known her older half brother?

Later, in the early-evening hours, Lauren finally got a look at the birdman, as she'd begun to think of her bizarre visitor.

And bizarre fit him to a T. Short and hugely overweight, the birdman wore a fabulous fur coat, which only served to make him appear even more massive. A retro-looking fedora sat low over his forehead, and the head beneath showed a gleaming absence of hair.

Gray eyes peered out from behind tiny John Lennon glasses. A pencil-thin Clark Gable mustache lined his narrow lips, and multiple chins rested on the dark tufts of what looked like sable. A carved silver walking stick hung over his left forearm.

"Hey, doll," he said, his high-pitched voice at odds with his vast bulk. "I'll take the bird now."

Before Lauren got even one word out, she felt David's solid warmth at her back. She glanced over her shoulder and gasped. His expression spelled out a warning. A shiver shot down her spine.

"And we have the *pleasure* of speaking with . . . ?" he asked.

Birdman blinked. "Me."

Just behind her, she felt David coil tight like a spring. "I'm sure you can do better than that," he said, menace in his words.

The birdman's thin lips almost vanished at his irritation. "Aloysius Dudley Rappaport, okay?"

Lauren fought a laugh. If he was an Aloysius anything, she had to be Phyllis Diller in full show garb.

"So, Aloysius, how about you tell us all about this bird of yours."

His eyes widened. "The bird's not mine," he squeaked. "It — it's Ric's. I made plans to pick it up here, but I . . . ah . . . got held up. But I'm here now. And I want it. Now."

"This bird must be pretty important."

"Oh, yeah."

"You know, Aloysius," David ventured.

107

"We have no idea what you're talking about. There's no bird in this house, and we've been on the hunt all day. Can you describe Ric's bird to us? Maybe that way we'll have a better idea what to look for."

"Ah . . . well, it's . . . er . . . it's big. A big bird, not only in size."

Lauren chuckled, despite her lingering fear. "That doesn't help much. Especially, since I never knew my brother to have any pets, and certainly not during the three years I lived here."

"Never said it was a pet, now did I?"

David placed a big palm on the door frame and leaned over Lauren's head. "I suggest you quit the games here — whatever your name is. We don't have a bird, and we don't know what you're up to."

The large man huffed, but he did step back. "Who'd you think you are, coming on with a threat like that? I'll have you know —"

"All you need to know is that I can make good on my threat, and you won't like it when I do."

"Well, if you're going to be that way . . ." He turned and headed down the steps. "I'll just have to call that lousy Ric DiStefano —"

Lauren gasped. "But —"

David's hand on her shoulder stopped her cold. "So you're going to call Ric."

The birdman, who'd stopped when Lauren gasped, shrugged. "Sure thing. I'm going to give him what-for. What's this stupid deal, sending me here, and you telling me there's no bird? He has the bird, he told me to come get the bird, I come get the bird, and you tell me there's no bird. Bah! You're all crazy, every one of you."

This time, as Aloysius lumbered to the sidewalk, David didn't call him back. Lauren realized she'd begun to tremble, and her knees felt weak.

He'd threatened to call Ric. Was —

"Lock the doors." David's voice allowed no argument. "Make sure none of you gets near a window. I'll be back."

Before she could say a word, he'd slipped past her, down the steps, and across the street. He got into an ordinary gray midsize sedan, and pulled out into traffic about three or four cars behind Aloysius's mint-condition vintage Pacer.

She didn't know whether to breathe a sigh of relief, since David was on the job, or whether to grab Mark and leave, find a hiding place where all the insanity wouldn't touch them again.

But something told her she had nowhere

to run. No matter where she went, this . . . this whatever it was would follow. She had no idea why.

But she did know one thing.

It was all about Ric.

Her dead brother.

Or was he?

David lost Aloysius about forty-five minutes later. Philly traffic was nothing to sneeze at. He pounded the steering wheel in frustration then looped on his cell phone's hands-free headset.

One ring later, he heard, "Prophet, here."

"Can you do me a favor, J.Z.?"

"Depends on what you want me to do."

"It's no biggie. I just need you to run down a name and a license plate number for me."

"Okay. Shoot."

David recited the number he'd memorized during his chase. Then, "And the guy's name is — you won't believe it, but it's what he said — Aloysius Dudley Rappaport."

"You've got to be joking."

"Not me, but I'm pretty sure he was."

"This have to do with the DiStefano woman?"

"Our pal Aloysius came to her front door looking for a bird. I looked for myself, and there's no bird there. She insists there never has been. See if when you check him out, you can find a reason, any reason, for his interest in feathered friends."

"A bird. Your Aloysius Dudley Rappaport wants a bird. From Ric DiStefano's sister —"

"Actually," David cut in, "Aloysius came to get the bird from Ric DiStefano, on DiStefano's invitation — or order. At least, that's what he told us."

"If you say so." J.Z. chuckled. "I just can't see DiStefano as any kind of an ornithologist."

"Neither can I. That's why I need you to get the scoop on this guy."

"I'll get back to you."

"Make it quick. I have a bad feeling about this."

By the time David made it through the tangle of traffic, another half hour had gone by. A sense of urgency kept him on edge, not at all like his normal, even-keeled nature. He didn't like it.

Everything revolved around DiStefano. And David knew, without a shadow of a doubt, that Lauren and Mark were in danger. That "accident" had left a bad taste in his mouth.

As he dodged a yellow taxicab in a hurry

111

to get nowhere fast in the bumper-to-bumper traffic, David thought of his buddy Walker Hopkins at the Securities and Exchange Commission. DiStefano had been under investigation for some fuzzy business practices. That had to be as good a place as any to start to dig into Lauren's brother's secrets.

Five minutes later, Walker had agreed to sift through everything related to DiStefano, and hoped to have the info ready in thirty-six to forty-eight hours.

"Shoot for thirty-six," David urged.

"Something big coming down?"

"I'm not sure, but Eliza assigned me to keep an eye on his family, a sister and his little boy. Someone tried to take them out a couple of days ago."

Walker's low whistle served to crank up David's anxiety. "Now you know how I feel."

"I'm on it, okay?"

"Sounds good," David said. "I'll tell you more when you get back to me."

They ended the conversation with a promise to get together soon. David yanked the headset off, flicked on his favorite classic jazz station, and wove in and out of traffic as fast as the law — and other drivers — allowed.

Finally, he turned the corner to Lauren's street. And not a moment too soon.

Despite his closed windows, despite the mellow music, despite the sound of the car that drove by in the opposite direction, David heard the unmistakable *rat-a-tat-tat-tat-tat-tat-tat-tat* of a Mac 10 automatic weapon.

He stomped on his brakes. Through the squeal of rubber against the road he also heard the crisp clatter of shattered glass. He opened the car door and ran, his own weapon drawn.

David saw no one up or down either side of the street.

But he did see the damage the gunman's bullets had done all too well. Things had just taken a turn for the worse.

Lauren's front windows had been shot out.

EIGHT

David ran up to the house, tried the door handle, and when he found it locked, pummeled the solid wood slab with his fist.

"Lauren, Gram . . . Mark! Open up, it's me."

Although he didn't blame them for not rushing to the door after what had just happened, the seconds felt like hours while he waited. "Come on, come on, *come on!*"

After what seemed a minor eternity, the door opened up a crack. In the gap, he saw Lauren's marble-pale face. "David?" she whispered.

"Yes, let me in." His relief was short-lived. "You're hurt! Didn't I tell you before I left not to get close to the windows? Seems my warning was prophetic."

The small, bloodied cut on her forehead didn't appear to trouble her. She straightened as if stuck with a pin. "Prophetic? Maybe. Or maybe you knew what was coming at me. How do I know that FBI identification you flashed around isn't a fake?"

"Bing-bing-bing! Give the lady the big teddy bear. She outed me. I'm Jim Carrey, master of the ridiculous."

He shook his head in disgust. "Give me a break. You watched me give it to a couple of cops, remember? They're trained to pick out fakes. You really think the Philly PD is in cahoots with me to fake you out? Why? Why would they — we — bother?"

She shrugged. "I don't know why you do anything. I don't know you."

"Okay. I can't quibble with that. But I don't know you, either. How do I know you're not part of some elaborate plot? The car accident, all that crazy bird stuff, now this blown-out window stunt . . . who's to say you aren't part of some bizarre gig?"

Her eyes gave off sparks again. "*I* say so. Besides, I'm no martyr wannabe. The bumps and bruises weren't life threatening, but they weren't fun, either. And I'm not happy about the vandalized windows. I'll probably have to sell this place, sooner rather than later, and to replace all that glass will cost me more than I have. Not to mention this."

She touched her forehead and winced.

A pang of guilt struck David. "Okay," he

said. "Maybe you aren't involved. But you have to admit something pretty weird is going on here."

Her nod came after long, silent moments. "I can't deny that. And from what I can see, it's all about my brother."

"That about sums it up."

"It seems I didn't know him as well as I thought I did."

"What do you mean?"

"None of what's happened makes sense. I don't know either of the odd characters that have come looking for him — or the bird, for that matter. My life here has been quiet, comfortable, and focused on Mark. All this . . . all of this is as foreign to me as outer space would be."

"So you're not part of all this. What does that have to do with knowing your brother?"

"The bizarre events began after Ric died. The car accident. The peculiar men who came to look for Ric or Ric's nonexistent bird, for that matter. And while Ric always told me he was a complete mess, the room I entered this morning was that of an obsessive neat freak."

David nodded. "Go ahead and toss the lack of funds into the mix while you're at it."

"True. I always understood him to be

more than solvent. After all, this —" she gestured to encompass her surroundings "— isn't the home of a man on the brink of bankruptcy."

"Now you get the picture."

"No. I only see a handful of puzzle pieces. And I can't put them together in a pattern that makes sense."

"I'll buy that." He ran a hand through his hair. "Let's go sit, okay? My adrenaline rush just rushed out of me. It's not an everyday thing to drive up to where I last saw my grandmother and find some animal shooting out all the glass on the place."

"You're telling *me* it got to *you?*"

The look on her face defied description, it was so full of disbelief, outrage and disdain. As she went into the parlor, she added, "Let me tell you, Mr. Latham, you have no idea what it was like on my side of that creep's spree."

He dropped into the comfortable curve of the sectional. "I've been shot at before."

She took the loungy end. "So it's all in a day's work."

"Something like that." He looked around. "Where'd you stash my grandmother and Mark?"

"You know? I'm not sure they even heard the shots. They've been in the basement since you left. This is an old house, built with thick, solid walls. Sound doesn't travel well, especially down toward the foundation."

"Thank you, Lord."

She slanted him a look. "This isn't the first time you've spoken of God. Are you a believer?"

"Have been for most of my life. And I have Gram to thank for that. My father had strayed from the faith, and my mom came from an agnostic family. We always spent part of our summer vacation in Philly, and Gram and Gramps had us in church whenever the door was open. My Sunday school teacher led a bunch of us to the Lord back when I was five or six."

"How wonderful!" Her smile dispelled a lot of the fear from when he first heard the shots. "And your parents?"

"Are you kidding? You've seen Gram in action. Who can hold out against that determined force?"

Lauren laughed. "I'd like to think they answered Christ's call."

"And whose voice did He choose to use?"

"Good point. She's wonderful, you know."

"The best."

And the best marched into the parlor right then. "Davey!" she said. "You're back.

That's nice. But what on earth are you two up to? I heard the strangest sound, like a rush of tinkly cymbals or maybe some kind of bells."

David met Lauren's gaze. He shrugged. "Nothing. We're innocent. But you did miss something —"

"Now would you just look at that? How did you break that lovely, lovely window? Were you bickering again? Lauren, dear, did you hit the end of your rope and toss something at my exasperating grandson? I know he tempts me often enough."

Lauren smiled. "No —"

"I wish she *had* pitched a fit," David said. "But no. The sounds of an automatic weapon and breaking glass welcomed me back. Someone shot out all the windows out front."

"Davey! You have to do something. This poor woman is in a very angry person's crosshairs. And that precious little boy! You can't just leave them at the mercy of the crazies."

"Guess what, Gram? I'm on the job, okay? Lauren and Mark *are* my assignment."

"And you're doing such a fine job of it, aren't you?" she said with a ton of sarcasm.

Lauren went to his irate grandmother. "I don't think you can fault him, Grandma

Dottie. He left to follow Aloysius — the birdman — and he couldn't have known that another lunatic would show up while he was gone."

His grandmother crossed her arms and struck her most pigheaded pose. "I don't see why not. Someone tried to run you over, right? He didn't succeed, so what makes the two of you think he'd give up just because?"

She had a point, but something from that night still stuck to the back of David's mind. "So Lauren, any more sightings of your brother's ghost? That is who you said was behind the car's wheel, right?"

She tipped up her nose. "And I told you I'd been under a great deal of stress. I'm also grieving the loss of my brother."

"So now you want me to believe it was all a figment of your imagination."

"No. There is a grave, and I know what I saw —"

"You're going to stick with the ghost deal, then." He shook his head. "Gotta tell you, I'm not buying your ghost story. From where I'm sitting, it sure looks like you have something to hide."

"I won't dignify that ignorant comment with a response."

"Okay, then. Sounds like I got it right. All

you can give is a nonanswer to my theory. Are you hiding your not-so-totally dead brother?"

"You have overstayed your welcome, Mr. Latham. Please leave."

"No can do. Have to get some of the boys in blue here to see about your potshot-happy visitor. And I am on the case. I'm going to stick to you like gum to the bottom of a running shoe. Before I'm done, I'm going to know just what you're hiding and why."

"Trust me. You already know what I'm hiding — nothing. And watching me is going to be a waste of your time. You should be going after the shooter or the driver of the Lexus. Even Aloysius bears watching. You'll get more answers out of them than me."

"Oh, I haven't given up on them. I'll get around to them soon enough. But first I'm going to find out what really happened out on that street, why weirdos come calling on you on a regular basis, whether your brother is dead or alive — and I'm also going to know why you're so determined to convince me that you see ghosts."

"You know what, Davey?" his grandmother said. "You're an idiot. Never thought I'd say that, but it's true. Quit badgering

Lauren and get back to work. Bring *us* some answers. That's what you do best."

"Much as I love you, Gram, I have no trouble telling you how gullible you are. I'm not going to fall for a pair of pretty green eyes or a cute little kid. She's up to something."

Before either woman could say anything more, David flipped open his cell phone and called police. Backup would arrive in no time. They'd look into the shooting.

He'd look after Lauren DiStefano.

That's where the answers lay.

Lauren was glad to see the police. At least it wasn't just her and David, still facing off. She'd had to fight to keep her temper under control. How could he think Ric was still alive? And how dare he ask her if she was hiding her brother?

She had little to offer the officers in the way of information. She'd been up in Ric's room, going through some flat boxes she'd found stored under the king-size bed. And in spite of the house's solid construction, she'd heard the gunshots and the breaking glass.

The officers left when they exhausted their barrage of questions. Lauren went straight back to the kitchen, grabbed the phone book and began to call handymen. She needed those windows boarded or they'd freeze overnight.

Partway down the list, after calling three or four with no success — too many jobs stacked up — she came across a company owned by a woman. When she explained her situation, Sophie Douglas offered sympathetic murmurs and promised to be right over.

Then Lauren turned her attention to the next immediate need. One way or another, she was going to have to hang in there long enough to concoct a meal. But when she began to rummage in the freezer, Grandma Dottie marched into the kitchen and overruled her efforts.

"It's a blessing the Lord planted me here today." She gave Lauren a gentle nudge. "Go on. Go lie down for a while. I'm here, I'm in charge, and I declare tonight pizza night."

The day had completely drained her. Lauren didn't even try to come up with an objection. "Pizza sounds wonderful. Thank you so much for everything you've done for us."

"Pshaw! I haven't done anything to speak of. Let's concentrate on helping Davey lock up the loonies. Then we can talk about

123

thanks and all that kind of thing."

Lauren went up to her room without another word. She collapsed on her bed and, in spite of the million thoughts whirling through her head, fell asleep right away.

Much too soon, she awoke to David's voice outside her bedroom door. "Pizza's here."

"I'm hungry, Aunt Lauren. Grandma Dottie says we hafta eat together. Pleeeeeze hurry."

She did, but on the way down the stairs, David laid a hand on her arm. "Hold on a minute, please."

Once Mark ran into the kitchen, she turned to David. "What —"

"I need to apologize for the way I acted earlier. Gram was right. I have no real reason to think you've withheld information, but I tore into you."

She shrugged, but didn't bother to respond.

He went on. "It didn't take me a whole lot of time to figure out that we'll get much further if we work together. Are you willing to help me?"

"As long as Mark is safe and you don't confuse me with a bug to put under your figurative microscope, then fine. I'll work with you. But you'll have to work with me, too. I have to know what's happening."

She watched him wrestle with her request. Eventually, though, he nodded. "I guess I don't have much choice, and no excuse not to let you know what I learn — as long as it doesn't jeopardize the investigation."

"Believe me. I don't want to interfere. I just need to understand what's going on at least as much as you do."

He held out his hand. "Truce then."

She took it, and noted its strength and warmth. "Truce."

The grin he shot her came full of mischief. "Then let's go break tomato-smeared bread, okay? I'm as hungry as Mark."

"And after dinner, I could use your help upstairs. I don't know where to start going through the masses of paperwork I found in Ric's room."

"You have yourself a deal."

Pizza with the Lathams was fun. Grandma Dottie and David kept up a running stream of love-filled banter. Lauren envied them their relationship. At times like this she missed her parents more than ever. And the look on Mark's face was priceless. She thanked the Lord for blessing her nephew with this small glimpse of strong family ties.

After the meal, she and David made their way to Ric's room. The look on the FBI agent's face when he took in the unbeliev-able volume of boxes would take a long time to forget.

She chuckled. "Impressive, don't you think?"

"Insane is what it is!" He turned a slow circle. "Why? Why would he pile up his room like this? How could he have slept in this loading dock?"

"I couldn't begin to say."

"But he was your brother, and you lived here, in his home."

Lauren shrugged. "Ric was twelve years older than me. That didn't make for a close relationship. And he was never a very af-fectionate man. I mean, he did love me and our parents, but he wasn't the kind who gave spontaneous hugs, and he rarely called."

"He must have been affectionate enough to fall in love, marry and have a son."

"Of course, he was. And you know? After he married Shelley, he did seem more relaxed — the few times I saw him."

"How about when you moved in?"

"Well, by then Shelley was dead, and he was a changed man."

"How so?"

"He'd always traveled for business, but when I moved in, he seemed desperate to escape his memories. He took back-to-back business trips all the time. He was rarely home."

David nodded. "That wouldn't help bring you any closer together."

"Exactly. And he was very involved with his Mummers' club."

"He was into the New Year's Day thing?"

"He belonged to one of the fancy clubs — you know, the ones with the huge, sparkly costumes."

"Not one of the street bands or a clown brigade, then."

Lauren laughed. "You wouldn't even ask that if you'd known Ric. He was as far from a clown as a man could be."

"So this serious businessman spent his free time putting together a lavish costume to parade up Broad Street on New Year's Day to the tune of 'Dem Golden Slippers.' "

"That sums it up pretty well."

"I don't get those guys, you know?" He shook his head, bemused. "Sure, the parade's a whole lot of fun to go and watch. We always came to Philly for Christmas, and Gram and Gramps never missed a parade. But to spend all that time putting together some crazy costume just to march up Broad Street . . . I don't know. I don't get it."

"You mean I won't see you anytime soon dressed in sequins and lamé?"

David laughed. "If I wasn't so sure you were teasing, I'd have you eat those words."

"On tomato-smeared bread, right?

"With mozzarella on top!"

On that upbeat note, they turned to the boxes. "How do you want to do this?" Lauren asked.

"I'm not even sure what we're looking for." He rubbed his temples with one broad hand. "Maybe it's going to be one of those we'll-know-it-when-we-see-it deals."

She groaned. "Then you're going to tell me we have to go through all of this."

He winked. "Stop it! I'm telling you, you're getting too good at reading my mind. Just stop it. I'm supposed to be inscrutable, you know, a blank slate, a rock wall. I'm an —"

"You're a spook, as Grandma Dottie says."

"Them's fightin' words, lady. Plus you joined my side."

"Then let's just fight the boxes."

He made a funny face. "Oh. Yeah. You're right. That's what we're supposed to do up here. Let's get started with this one right here, then, Ms. Party Pooper."

"With that kind of enthusiasm, we're really going to get far."

He dropped down by the box he'd pointed to at the foot of the bed. "Did I ever tell you I'm not a paper-pusher?"

"That's pencil-pusher."

"Same difference." He pulled a wad of papers from the box. "You have to push the pencil across paper, right?"

Lauren rolled her eyes and took a stack of her own. "You're a little odd, you know?"

"So I've been told, most often by my grandmother —"

His long whistle caught her off guard. "What's wrong?" she asked.

"I'm not sure yet that anything's wrong, but if these figures are right, your brother was swimming in dough." He met her gaze. "So where is the dough?"

Lauren leaned over, looked at the list of entries he'd just checked. "Millions?"

"That's what this says."

She sat back on her heels. "I have no idea. Last I knew, Ric had almost a million dollars in outstanding debt. His life insurance policy is for one million. That's why I have to look at putting the house on the market in the new year."

He turned back to the pertinent page. "This is about a year old, so unless he hit a bad downturn since then, he was doing spectacular business."

Lauren sighed. "We really do have to go through all this."

He grinned. "Get to work, woman. We don't have a moment to lose."

She sent him a mock frown. "Don't push your luck. I'm helping you already, but if you don't play nice . . . Just remember, Mr. FBI Agent Man, you're not the boss of me!"

"Yeah, yeah, yeah. But the sooner we get to work here, the sooner we'll be done."

They turned back to their respective paperwork, and continued to sort through business records for the next two hours. The only thing that broke the silence was David's occasional mutters.

"Why didn't he just use software to keep records? Look at all the trees he could've saved. It'd be so much quicker to just scan a computer file."

Lauren chuckled, but didn't respond. She just continued to examine documents. But now that she'd seen — and understood — what the figures meant on the paper David had found, she went through the masses of dates more thoroughly.

That's why when, after three whole boxes of paperwork, she found a much more recent version of that earlier revealing statement, she knew what she held in her hand.

"David," she said, her nerves on edge.

"Look at this. I think I've found something."

"Let me see." He took the paper, stared at it for a long time. Then he looked at her, met her gaze.

"This just backs up some information the Bureau has. On paper, your brother was making money hand over fist. But you say you have evidence that he was virtually broke. It's no wonder the SEC — the Securities and Exchange Commission — was looking into his business."

Lauren's stomach dropped. "Ric was being investigated? What for?"

"Fraud, unethical transactions, illegal business practices."

Her world began to spin. She felt cold, dizzy, off-kilter. She could no longer distinguish between what was real and what was not. Only one thing seemed clear. She hadn't known her brother very well after all.

"Why?" she asked in a whisper. "Why would he be involved in something like that?"

"That's what we don't know. What we need to find out."

"And all this other business, the car accident, the strangers who want something from him, the shot-out windows, its all part of it, isn't it?"

131

He nodded. "And we have to figure it out before —"

At his abrupt stop, Lauren figured she'd wait for him to continue. When he didn't, she said, "Before what?"

He looked up at her, his hazel eyes boring into hers, as if he might find his answers somewhere inside her. "Before the people who want to hurt you succeed."

She winced. "What you really mean is before the people who want to kill me succeed."

He didn't deny her words.

NINE

Why? Why would anyone want to kill her?

Lauren couldn't figure that one out. Not only had she not known anything about Ric's business, but she also knew none of his friends and acquaintances. What would make a stranger want her dead?

After David had left, she'd turned to her Bible and prayer. Now she lay in bed, physically exhausted, but mentally wide-awake. And she didn't want to think anymore, at least not about what had happened.

After about one hour of fighting her thoughts, she turned to her bedside radio, found her favorite classical station and set the volume to a gentle hum. She lay on her back, purposely relaxed her body from her toes to her head, took deep and even breaths, and kept a Scripture verse in mind.

Peace I leave with you; my peace I give you . . .

All Lauren wanted for Christmas was a

good measure of the Lord's peace.

David approached the DiStefano mansion with a healthy case of misgiving. Hey, the last time he'd come here, some jerk had shot out all the glass across the front of the house.

He'd touched base with J.Z. and Walker Hopkins at the SEC. They'd agreed that more eyes would only help. While J.Z. was busy with an investigation of his own, Walker had access to the file his colleagues had been working on for a while — and he had enough seniority to get himself assigned to the case.

He couldn't wait for Lauren's reaction when she came face-to-face with his pal Walker. He knew the huge grin he couldn't contain would probably surprise her, but he figured they could both use a bit of cheer. He ran up the front steps and rang the doorbell.

"Are you going to let me in on the joke?" she asked, when she opened the door.

The dark bruise on her forehead made him feel like a heel. "No joke, and I'm really sorry about yesterday. Especially because you were hurt."

She touched the spot, and couldn't mask the pain. "I'm okay, David. It wasn't your

134

fault. Some crackpot out there is the one who took up a weapon, came out here, did damage and got me with a piece of the glass he shattered."

David clamped down on his jaw. "Yes, but my job is to protect you."

She arched a brow. "Among other things, right?"

That skeptical look, the slightly ironic smile, and her tousled blond hair caught his attention in a brand-new way. He realized how pretty Lauren DiStefano was.

"No comment, huh?"

David's cheeks turned up the heat. "Uh . . . sorry. I was thinking . . . um . . . yes. Sure. I do have to figure out what your brother was up to. And I need to make sure you and Mark are safe."

"Don't fudge around the truth, David. What you have to do is make sure you keep Mark and me alive."

"That, too."

Just then Mark barreled into the foyer. "Monster Man! Wanna play with Ochiban?"

David turned to Lauren. "Ochiban?"

She smiled. "Go ahead, Mark. Show Mr. Latham what you mean."

Mark pulled a small, black gadget from his pocket, and something whirred down the hallway from the kitchen.

And it was something all right. A silver bullet shaped . . . thing, about eighteen inches high, rolled up and gave off a bunch of beeps. "What on earth is *that?*"

Lauren laughed. "That's Ochiban, Mark's robot friend."

David scratched his chin. "A robot. What does a kid need a robot for? And what does it do?"

"Aw, Monster Man. Ochiban is great," Mark said. "Come see."

David took the boy's outstretched hand and let himself be dragged into the parlor. Ochiban followed.

For the next fifteen minutes Mark and Ochiban amazed him. The little machine performed a number of simple tasks, and anyone could see it had stolen Mark's heart.

"D'you like my friend?" the boy asked after Ochiban's performance.

"He is pretty cool."

"Uh-huh! My daddy got him for me on a trip."

The boy's innocent reference to Ric crashed David back to reality. "That's some souvenir, kiddo. But now I have to get back to work."

"What work d'you do?"

David stared at that innocent face. Could he tell Mark what he really did? Would that be in the boy's best interest? He doubted it.

But before he had a chance to stick his foot in his mouth, Lauren walked in. "Why don't you go to the kitchen and bring us the plate with cookies, Mark? I'm sure Mr. Latham would like a couple of them."

"Yum!" the boy yelled and took off.

"Don't run and be careful!" she added.

Once they were alone, David turned to Lauren. "So your brother didn't find the my-daddy-went-to-Tokyo-and-all-I-got-was-this-lousy-T-shirt present good enough for Mark."

She shrugged. "I'm not sure he gave presents a whole lot of thought. Everything he brought back, for Mark and me, was exquisite and extravagant. I think that on some level Ric tried to make up for his absence by showering us with gifts."

"How about money? You did give up your job to take care of him and his son. What have you done for personal funds?"

"Ric paid me a salary for the housekeeping. It wasn't as much as I made teaching, but it was adequate since I didn't have to pay for my living expenses."

"And that salary disappeared when Ric died."

She nodded.

"How are you set for money right now?"

"I've never been very extravagant, not like Ric. I saved a good amount of my teaching salary and almost everything Ric paid me. I have enough to see Mark and me through until I get a new job, but I certainly can't pay for the destroyed windows. Last I checked, home insurance was paid and up-to-date. Plus Ric's life insurance policy —"

"I remember. You said that would just about cover the debts he left behind."

"That pretty much sums it up. Which means you and I have to get back to that mess upstairs."

"That's not a mess, Lauren. If you think that's a mess, then you've lived a very sheltered life. That room's the neatest records warehouse I've ever seen. But in these days of superbrainy computers, I don't understand why Ric didn't make use of the technology."

"Maybe we'll find out why when we go through the boxes."

He didn't think so, but he didn't want to argue. "Either way, it's time to get back to the salt mines."

"You slave driver, you."

"And don't you forget it."

They went up to the third floor, utility knife in hand, and resumed their rummaging through Ric DiStefano's things. David kept an ear out for Walker, but for the most part the house remained quiet. The plywood over the broken window gave the room an eerie feel, and their only interruption came from Mark's frequent visits.

Finally, after two hours of boring paper-work, the doorbell rang. Lauren stood. "I'll go get that."

David knew who most likely had arrived, but he didn't want to tip her off. He couldn't wait to watch the meeting. "I'll come with you. My legs can stand to stretch."

His expectations weren't dashed. Lauren opened the door to a six-foot-eleven black man, whose deep eyes were topped with thick, straight brows and nothing else. Walker's head glistened like fresh-poured chocolate glaze.

Her gaze went from his shoes all the way to what Walker called his "cocoa dome." As her eyes moved up, her jaw gaped down.

"I'm Walker."

Lauren blinked. "Ah . . . I'm Lauren. What . . . how can I help you?"

"No, ma'am," David's friend said, his military background evident in the respect he put in the two words. "I'm here to help you."

She stepped back. "I don't need help —"

139

He stepped forward. "Begging your pardon, ma'am. But that's not what I hear."

"I don't need a bouncer!" Then she must have realized what she'd said. "Oh, no! I'm sorry. I didn't mean that the way it came out."

"You must know I'm not a bouncer, Ms. DiStefano."

"I don't know a thing about you. You could be the next Picasso or Mikhail Baryshnikov, but that wouldn't mean a thing to me."

David couldn't choke back his laugh. "That's the first time anyone's ever accused him of being an artsy kind of guy. Michael Jordan? Maybe. But a painter or a dancer? Never!"

Lauren spun to face him. "Is this your idea of a joke — wait! That's why you were laughing when you got here this morning. You set me up."

Walker crossed his arms. He stared at David, sent him a clear message. "You didn't tell her I'm on the job?"

The average man would be intimidated by Walker's superior height and solid bulk. But David had known the guy since college days, and while a nine-inch difference separated the tops of their heads, their friendship erased any possible weirdness.

He stuck his hands in his pockets. "Sure didn't. I couldn't wait to see you do your thing you do so well."

Lauren's gaze ping-ponged between them. Walker looked confused. "But I haven't done a thing."

"That's what I love most about you, pal. You're all natural."

The Lord had blessed Walker with an impressive frown. "You're a mean man, Latham."

"And you're an overgrown teddy bear. But you still have a whopper effect on everyone you meet."

"You going to start with those dumb puns again?" Walker asked. " 'Cause if you are . . ." He turned to Lauren. "Don't you worry ma'am, I'm here to rescue you from this clown's pathetic efforts."

Lauren turned from Walker to stare at David. "Clown? Are you telling me you think he's *funny?*"

"No, ma'am. That's just it. He's a frustrated, misguided soul. He's *not* funny, even though he thinks he is."

Lauren crossed her arms, and while her bulk didn't have the oomph Walker's did, her glare made David a whole lot uneasier than his friend's scowls ever had.

"Uh-oh," he said.

Walker laughed.

Lauren didn't. "Okay, gentlemen — and that old cliché about using the term loosely is applicable here — it's obvious you know each other, but I'm in the dark. How about we start all over?"

"Yeah, Davey," Walker said. "How about you start all over again, and this time do it right?"

"Sure thing, Scrooge." David turned to Lauren. "Lauren DiStefano, allow me to introduce my college roommate, Walker Hopkins. The guy's an accounting genius. Not even a stray penny gets by him, which is why the Securities and Exchange Commission pays him the big bucks."

Walker snorted. "Sure thing, Special Agent Latham. We both work for the government, so if I'm getting the big bucks, then so are you."

"Time out!" Lauren cried. "*I'm* going to tell *you* what *we're* going to do now. You both will give your vocal cords a break, while I try and translate what I think I heard you say."

Walker met David's gaze, shrugged, grinned, and then faced Lauren again. David chuckled. Lauren DiStefano was a fascinating woman.

The fascinating woman began to speak. "I

142

can safely assume Mr. Hopkins is here, not to visit his college pal, but to look into my brother's financial dealings. I can also assume that Mr. Latham called Mr. Hopkins because he felt Mr. Hopkins would do a better job of tracking down the missing millions than he can. How am I doing, gents?"

"She's pretty smart, Dave —"

"What's Davey smart about? And what are you doing out on the front step?" David's grandmother asked as she marched up the front walk. "Haven't you noticed that winter's here? It's cold!"

David groaned.

Walker exclaimed, "Grandma!"

Lauren stared at David's grandmother, confusion on her face. "I'm glad you're here, Grandma Dottie. Maybe you can make sense of them."

Gram stomped up the steps, reached up to yank Walker's ear, then hugged him. "You're lucky I love both of you, but I know just how Lauren feels. Around them, honey, you have to pinch yourself every so often. They're a pair of characters, but deep down, they're okay."

"Hmm . . . sounds as though I'm going to need to sharpen a shovel. I'll have to dig a long while to find that deep, down okay."

David narrowed his eyes. "Where'd this

brand-new, smart-mouthed Lauren Di-Stefano come from? The Lauren I left here last night was sweet, soft-spoken and scared."

The green fire in her gaze again caught him by surprise. Had he completely misread her? Was she the kind of woman that old cliché about hidden depths described? If so, he was in trouble.

"Would you believe, Mr. Latham, that I'm sick and tired of all the strange things that have happened to me in the last few weeks? I'm losing my patience, which I've always been told is vast. I have an enormous responsibility — I have to look out for Mark's well-being. All these threats have made me mad."

"Looks like you blew this one, dude." Walker chuckled. "Here I thought I was coming to rescue a shy schoolteacher, and now I'm wondering if you're the one I'm going to rescue in the end."

"No way, man. Beats me where you got this rescue idea. I've been on the job for a while now, and I'm the one who'll be doing all the rescue work around here. Remember you're here to do your numbers gig."

"Whoo-boy!" his grandmother said as she sailed into the home. "Lauren, my dear, if you were counting on Davey to rescue you, with the way things have come down, you're in more trouble than I thought. I don't know what's happened to him lately, but he's not doing the job he usually does. Just look at those windows, if you don't believe me."

Lauren shot a Walker-and-David-encompassing glare. "I don't need a rescuer. I need answers. And if either one of you can give me some, then I'll be immensely grateful. But since we've wasted enough time with your goofy games, Mr. Latham, then I suggest we head upstairs and get to work."

"Mr. Latham, huh?" Walker asked with a grin. "Awfully formal, Dave. Sounds to me like the lady's not too fond of you."

"Right now his grandmother's not too fond of him. What kind of games has he been playing?"

Green eyes slanted toward him. "I wouldn't even call them games. I'd say he has a sophomoric streak he likes to indulge."

"Hey! That was not nice." But his assignment ignored his objection and marched up the elegant stairs, her slender right hand on the intricately carved handrail. She struck David as the epitome of vintage feminine dignity.

He was in trouble.

Gram chuckled. "Know what, Davey? You'd better open your eyes. She's a keeper, and if you wise up, you might just win yourself the prize."

"You, Gram, are nuts." His stomach felt weird, though, and multiple images of Lauren ran through his memory. To clear his mind of all the dangerous stuff, he turned to Walker.

"Time to work, man. You won't believe the mountains we have to go through."

His friend laid a hand on David's shoulder. "I wouldn't be in such a hurry, dude. You look guilty and scared. That's one interesting lady, and if she's as innocent as she's said, and which I suspect, then I have to agree with Grandma Dottie. Open up your eyes and look good and hard at what's before you."

David gave a disgusted snort on his way up the stairs. "About the smartest thing she's said is that it's time to get to work. Come on."

And they did get to work. Predictably, Walker flipped when he saw the boxes. But with a groan, he took one of the highest ones, brought it down to the floor and began to dig.

Walker's concentration took David back to college days. While he'd taken modern history and government courses in preparation for law school, Walker had spent hours muttering numbers in a wide variety of combinations. He did the same up on the DiStefano's third floor.

Lauren shot frequent leery looks at them, as if scared they'd go back into their odd couple routine. True, he shouldn't have set her up, but Walker always brought out his sense of the ridiculous. He'd have to apologize to Lauren — again. But not until after Walker was gone.

"Hmm . . ." Walker murmured just then.

The tone of the murmur caught David's attention. He looked at his friend. Lauren also turned to stare.

A few seconds later, the big man repeated himself, this time, his voice a deeper, resounding bass.

Curiosity burned in David's gut, but he knew to wait.

Lauren leaned closer to Walker, who didn't notice.

Another five minutes of torture went by before Walker looked up. "Have you seen this, Dave?"

"What?"

"This list of stock buys and sales."

"I've seen a bunch of them. DiStefano had a whole lot of clients. He did a truckload of transactions. Which ones are you talking about?"

He handed a piece of paper to David. "See if anything jumps out at you. It danced off the page at me."

David took the long sheet of paper, legal-pad length. Names ranged down the left side, single-spaced, and in small print. Directly across from the names, a series of figures suggested stock or securities purchases followed by sales. Along the right-hand edge of the paper, a list of totals showed extravagant gains, fortunes made.

But it wasn't the earnings that caught David's attention. They hadn't caught Walker's, either. Halfway down the list of clients, one particular, familiar name detonated alarm bells.

"Carlo Papparelli," David said.

"The Laundromat," Walker added.

"What are you talking about?" Lauren asked. "Who is that man? And what does he have to do with laundry?"

David met her gaze. "The only kind of laundry Papparelli ever did was of the totally illegal money kind. And he did it for the mob. He was shot, execution style, about six months ago. But he didn't die right away. He went into a nursing home, and his unhappy 'colleagues' got him there."

Her face lost its normal, peachy glow. "Why would his name be on Ric's records? What does it mean?"

Walker looked at her, sympathy on his face. "I think you have a pretty good idea, Ms. DiStefano. If it turns out that your brother regularly invested the Laundromat's dirty money, then he might have been 'connected,' too."

"Connected?"

David reached out and took hold of her icy hand. "Remember? I told you. Someone reported your brother to the Securities and Exchange Commission. That's why he was under investigation for alleged fraud."

Her fingers began to tremble.

Walker nodded. "That's not the worst of it. If he was investing Papparelli's dirty money, there's a good chance he knew more than just how much he was making for the mob."

"You mean . . ." She slanted David a horror-filled look. "Is he saying that my brother had something to do with the . . ."

David finished her sentence. "The mob."

"Oh, Lord Jesus," she said in a fervent voice. "No! Please, *please,* no, Father. No."

"You're 'sposed to be my friend, Monster Man!" Mark cried from the doorway. "But you're mean. Why'd you make Aunt

Lauren cry?"

The boy hurtled into his aunt's arms.

David met Walker's gaze. What could he say? He had no way to put the truth into words that wouldn't do harm to an innocent five-year-old.

As hard as the truth had hit the boy's adult aunt, he could only imagine how it might scar Mark if David told him his father could very well have been a mobster.

He felt the tug of Lauren's gaze. He turned and read her plea.

There was nothing he could do or say.

For once, they both agreed.

Mark mattered most.

TEN

The men left in the afternoon, not a minute too soon for Lauren. Her stomach had knotted when Walker found the incriminating name on Ric's records, her head had begun to pound, and she'd struggled to keep her attention on anything other than that.

Even now, her thoughts revolved around only one thing: the mob and her brother's potential connection to organized crime.

Could Ric really have been involved with those kind of people? Had he been part of that ugly, shadowy culture? Had he helped mobsters maximize their ill-gotten gains?

Was that why he'd never introduced her to his acquaintances?

How could her half brother have betrayed everything their father had stood for? She knew Ric was raised in the church, as was she. Her father had loved the Lord and made sure his children came to know the Father as well as he did.

Lauren went through the motions of making a meal. At her back, Mark kept up his normal stream of chatter. Every once in a while he scolded her for not listening, something she always insisted he do when she spoke.

"Aunt *Lauren*," he said in a frustrated voice. "Lissen! I wanna take Ochiban to show-and-tell. Can I? Can I, pleeeeze?"

After she'd learned about her brother's possible secret life earlier in the day, Lauren wanted nothing to do with a gift bought with dirty money. Especially if it turned out that Ric had lavished her and Mark with extravagances to distract her from his activities.

But she had no reasonable way to deny Mark. "When is the show-and-tell event?"

"Miss Green says Friday."

"I'm free that morning, so how about I talk to her when I pick you up from school tomorrow? I'll have to explain that I can't leave Ochiban there after you show him, okay? He's too expensive, and I don't think the school will want to be responsible for keeping him safe and unhurt."

"Aw, my friends won't hurt Ochiban. They just wanna play with him."

"I can stay with you so they can play for as long as they want — if your teacher lets me."

"Okay. Can you make cookies?"

Lauren tried to remember what ingredients she had left and what her checking account had added up to the last time she looked. She didn't want to go much more deeply into her savings until she absolutely had to, like for rent or food — the real thing rather than cookies or snacks.

"I think I have everything for chocolate chip cookies."

"Yum! My fav'rits."

The evening continued in the same vein. Lauren had never counted minutes as avidly as she did then. Seven-thirty, Mark's bedtime, seemed in no hurry to arrive.

But it finally did. She rushed their usual routine of bath, bedtime story, prayers, hugs, kisses and good night. Then she made herself go back downstairs rather than up to Ric's room. She wanted — no, needed — to know for certain what he had been involved with. But first she had to face the stack of envelopes the mailman had brought today. She hated sorting the bills, only because she didn't know where she'd get the money to pay them.

With a sigh, she slipped a selection of Gustav Holst's music in the CD player then plopped on the chaise part of the sectional, her hands full of mail, a pen and her checkbook.

The junk mail she dropped into the small woven reed trash can she kept at the side of the chaise. Most of the bills were the usual monthly ones, like utilities, phone, newspaper delivery. She paid those. Finally, when she could postpone it no longer, she faced the mortgage.

But the envelope turned out not to contain the usual statement. Instead, it brought her the letter she'd most dreaded. The bank had begun foreclosure proceedings.

Ric had handled all financial affairs, and Lauren never suspected the mortgage had gone unpaid. She only learned of the dismal situation when his death forced her to take over as the new head of the home. What she'd learned had shocked her.

Especially since she didn't have anywhere near the money to bring the payments up-to-date. And even though she'd tried to negotiate some kind of arrangement with the bank, hoping her brother's death would encourage the management to leniency, it seemed Ric hadn't had a stellar relationship with his financial institution.

Now she and Mark would reap what Ric had sowed.

Lauren struggled to contain her bitterness.

She filed the letter with the folder of information the Realtor she'd contacted had given her, and then, drained beyond belief, headed upstairs. As a Christian, she knew she had to turn everything over to the Lord, but this one was proving a challenge.

The first shock of her brother's death had hit her hard. Then she'd learned the dismal state of Ric's finances. Grief and a heartbroken little boy had consumed her days. Then today she was hit with the mob angle. And now she learned she and Mark would soon be homeless.

Anger came fast and easy. Peace? Not so much.

She tried to pray, but for the most part, her communication with the Father consisted of whys and how comes. Finally, after hours of hopeless cries for answers, she fell asleep.

Oncoming headlights filled her dreams.

"You're *what?*" David asked two days after Walker's visit to the DiStefano house.

"I'm moving out," Lauren answered.

How could she stand there and say something like that in such a calm, steady voice? Was she made of ice?

"Why?" he asked. "Where are you going to go? What's going to happen to you and Mark?"

"I'm moving because I have to list the house for sale. I'm not sure where we'll go, and I have no idea what's going to happen to us. I have to leave that in God's capable hands."

David spanned his forehead with thumb and middle finger, and rubbed. "Have you thought this through?"

"There's not a whole lot to think through, David. I got word that the bank's gone forward with the foreclosure. I can't pay what's owed, and I want to avoid losing what equity is in the home. I'm going to need every penny I can save for Mark's education. So I hope to sell quickly. Know of a cheap but safe place to rent?"

"Didn't Ric have mortgage insurance? That should cover the mortgage now that he's dead."

Lauren let out a humorless laugh. "We're lucky he had home owners and life insurance. That's all the money I've found so far."

"I want to know where all those millions went." He paced the length of the parlor. "Walker and the other SEC investigators on the case combed through most of that paperwork already, and nothing came up to lead us to the mother lode."

"Why do you think there is a mother

lode?" She crossed to the window, stared out at the gray, slushy street he'd navigated to get here. "If he was investing money for clients, then it belonged to them."

"Yes, but the commissions he cleared from those giant transactions were his. Where'd they go?"

She shrugged. "They don't help since I don't have them."

He followed the path he now thought would lead to some answers. "You said your brother traveled a lot. I asked one of my colleagues at the Bureau to check that out. Maybe Ric's trips will give us a clue."

"You think he banked his profits abroad?"

"Many have done that."

"It would explain the lack of funds." She sighed. "But why? Wouldn't he want to keep all that money where he could get to it fast and easy? It seems awkward to keep it that far away."

"As I said, it's been done by many. These days, electronic transfers move all the money anyone might want almost instantly."

She turned back to stare outside, arms around her middle, her shoulders slumped, the tumble of her golden honey curls shielding her face. When she spoke again, she didn't face him.

"It looks worse by the minute, doesn't it?"

"It really does."

Then she turned and met his gaze. "If you understand that, how can you ask why I have to sell this place? I can't pay the mortgage, even if someone hires me today."

"I'm sorry."

"It's not your fault."

"I know, but I feel bad for you."

"I'm not worried about me. It's Mark that concerns me."

"Me, too."

They fell silent again. David took in the contents of the comfortable, well-decorated room. "When do you plan to move?"

"As soon as I can pack and find a place to go."

"Sounds like a monster job for a woman with a child."

"I'll do what I have to do, Monster Man, and trust the Lord to see me through."

He grinned. "Tell you what. I have some friends I can count on. They'll give us a hand. You find a place to go, and we'll take care of the move."

"You don't have to do that —"

"I know I don't, but the Lord does call me to help those who need a hand. Besides, Walker would shoot me if I didn't call him —"

"How about if you don't make any more

comments like that?" She shuddered. "You know, the shooting thing. It's just too close for comfort right now."

How rotten could a guy feel? He went to her side. "I'm sorry. How's your forehead?"

She touched the small wound with a finger. "I'd pretty much forgotten about it. It's the thought of what the bullets could have done, especially to Mark, that chills me to the bone."

David couldn't resist touching her forehead. "It does seem to be healing well."

That's when her light, feminine, floral scent reached him. Sweet and delicate, it suited her to perfection and echoed the silky softness of her skin. David stumbled back, too aware of the danger Lauren DiStefano posed.

It had nothing to do with bullets, mobsters or hit-and-runs.

It had everything to do with broken hearts, mended hearts, throbbing hearts, and all that jazz. David was no poet; even less, a fan of mushy, industrial-size tissue box chick flicks.

"Ah . . . gotta go."

Oh, man! What eloquence. He blushed. "Um — er . . . I'll let you know if anything comes up. And I'll get the guys lined up. For the move, you know."

A frown drew two thin lines between her brows. "Is something wrong?"

Yes! "No! Of course not. I'm fine. Really. Never better. I . . . I just have to get back to work. To find out what happened with all that money, you know."

Skepticism splashed all over her face. He hadn't done himself any favors with his clumsy efforts. "Time to go. See ya."

He let himself out the door, ran down the steps as if the hound of the Baskervilles was on his heels, and decided Walker would have the pleasure of dealing with Lauren Di-Stefano from here on in. He'd still keep her under surveillance, but from a safe distance.

No matter what Eliza Roberts had to say about it.

Even if she chose to fire him.

Lauren was too dangerous to his health.

His heart's health.

Lauren drove to the Realtor's office, but once she came up to the building, she could find no parking for two and a half blocks up and down the street. With a resigned sigh, she pulled her subcompact into the nearest open spot, parked and headed to her destination by foot.

She hadn't gone more than a few feet

before she experienced a strange feeling. A look over her shoulder revealed nothing more than a man in a dark brown coat and orange knit stocking-style winter hat. He ambled up the sidewalk in no apparent hurry to get where he was headed.

It must be wonderful to be at such peace with the world.

Lauren picked up her pace. Since she'd had to park so much farther from the real estate office than she'd hoped, she had no time to waste. Even though she would rather be anywhere but headed there. She didn't really want to sell the house, Mark's home, but she saw no other way out of her situation.

At the corner, she waited for the pedestrian Walk sign to turn green. Smack in the middle of the intersection, she again felt that strange sensation. She glanced back, and this time saw two women, bloated shopping bags in hand just feet behind the same gentleman. Christmas shopping would be nice, but she didn't know how much she could afford to spend.

As she approached the real estate office, two men carrying a long, flat, and, from the strain on their faces, very heavy box, blocked the sidewalk. Lauren stopped and waited. Then everything turned into a surreal sequence of events, much like a movie, one in which she really wanted no part.

The men dropped the box, which broke and spewed small steel balls all over the sidewalk. Both tripped on their fleeing cargo. They landed in a tangle of arms and legs, howling and yelling at each other.

Lauren tried to dodge the tiny spheres, and would have done so if someone hadn't crashed into her from behind.

"Oh, no!" She flailed her arms, tried to regain her balance, but couldn't. She joined the men amid the treacherous steel balls.

The man who'd walked behind her down the sidewalk approached. She smiled her gratitude, and reached out a hand. But instead of helping her, he bent down, grabbed one of the steel balls, then knocked into her, straightened and started back on his way.

"Oh, no you don't, buddy boy!"

"Grandma Dottie!" Lauren cried, relieved.

David's grandmother yelled out a quick "Hello" then tackled the man in the brown coat.

Dottie looked over her shoulder. "Here's your handbag." Lauren's purse flew through the air. "Use your cell phone to call the cops. I got me a live crook here."

Only then, through the sting of scraped

knees and the fear in her heart, did she realize the man had stolen her bag. She narrowed her eyes, took a good look at the crook on whose back Grandma Dottie now perched, then made the call.

When done, but before she could ask any of the million questions in her head, a salt-and-pepper fluff-haired woman of Grandma Dottie's vintage trotted toward them.

"Good job, Dottie, dear," the short, wiry lady said. "That'll teach the creep not to . . ." She waved, clearly seeking a word. "Well, you know. Not to be . . . Oh, yeah, yeah! I got it. Not to be so — get this — scuzzy!"

Her grin spanned her narrow face. "How'd you like that one, Dot?"

"Awesome, Bea. Come help me squash this perp into a pulp."

"Good one, good one."

To Lauren's shock, Bea plopped down on the guy's legs, all the while keeping up a stream of slang with her pal. Each of the ladies tried to impress the other with her superior knowledge of contemporary vernacular, but neither seemed the least interested in why the man had tried to rob Lauren.

So she crawled over a ton of steel marbles and asked. "Why did you take my purse?

And why did you wait until I was down to do it?"

"Well, duh!" Grandma Dottie's Q-tip-shaped friend said. "When you're up and going, stealing you blind isn't so easy."

"I understand that. But he waited until he had a number of witnesses. It would have been easier, safer and smarter if he'd attacked when it was just the two of us on the sidewalk."

"She's right, Bea," David's grandmother said. "I followed them, and there was no one else around but the three of us."

She bounced on her captive's back. "So why'd you do it?"

The guy grunted, but didn't speak. Lauren doubted he could. "Don't you think he might need to breathe?"

Bea looked down in disgust. "I think he needs to suffer for his crimes."

Before Lauren could come up with something to say after that, sirens sounded close. A moment later, a crew of uniformed officers descended on the three women and three men. One cop helped Grandma Dottie to her feet. Another took statements from the fallen deliverymen. A third clapped handcuffs on the hapless purse snatcher, while a fourth asked Lauren what had happened.

A short time after the men in blue arrived, another car drove up. David jumped out and ran toward them. "Gram! Lauren! Are you okay?"

Grandma Dottie gave him an exasperated glare. "Of course, we're all right. We're no Victorian wilting lilies, you know."

"We are women, hear us roar!" Bea added then winked at Lauren. "We're no wimps."

Lauren had to smile. "Hi, David. Fancy meeting you here."

"No coincidence. These two —" he pointed to his grandmother and her friend "— have a long history with the Philly PD. The officers let me know whenever either one is involved in an 'incident.' "

"Your grandmother's got a rap sheet?"

"Not exactly." He slanted a look at the two seniors. "Let's just say Bea's driving doesn't quite line up with the laws of the State of Pennsylvania."

"Ah . . . a speed demon."

"And more."

Lauren laughed. "I guess it pays to have friends in high places."

"It's your only line of defense when you're related to Dorothea Stevens Latham."

"Hey, Davey, enough with the nasties," Grandma Dottie said. "Did you get a load of this guy's face? He looks a little like that

165

bird guy — Alpharetus . . . Alphonsius . . .
whatever."

"Aloysius, Gram. And no, I can't say I had
a chance to even look at the guy. Will you
three stay here — please don't move, okay?
— while I go talk to the officers?"

His grandmother snorted. "Feeling important, are we?"

"No, just concerned that one or all three
of you will jump up and find more trouble
to get into."

"Bogus!" Bea cried. "Don't go getting so
big for your britches, boy. I still remember
the day you hid a lit firecracker in your
pocket. It's not many kids who're so dumb
as to make their pants explode, you know."

Lauren laughed. "Now there's an image
for you, Mr. FBI Agent."

He glared then marched toward the officers who'd just stuffed the would-be purse
snatcher into one of the patrol cars. Lauren
watched David out the corner of her eye,
noted his intense expression, the clean lines
of his attractive face, the lean strength of his
tall frame, the certainty with which he carried himself.

After a brief conversation, he dipped down
and stuck his head inside the patrol car.
Then he straightened again, rapped the roof
of the car with his knuckles and returned to

the women's side, his expression serious.

"Good eye, Gram."

Grandma Dottie shrugged. "I got a good look at him when I tackled him. That's all. So what's the deal?"

"He's Aloysius's cousin Theodosius, Theodosius Bentley Witherspoon."

"Gesundheit!" quipped Bea. "What's wrong with Tom, Dick or Harry?"

Grandma Dottie tsk-tsked. "Even Bobby, Billy or Tommy would do just as well."

"Can we get real here?" David said. "Lauren's in danger, and that means Mark's in danger, too. Plus she's selling her house. We have people to see, places to go."

"You're selling that beautiful house?" Grandma Dottie's dismay laced her words. "Oh, Lauren, dear. Why?"

"Because I have to. I can't afford to keep it."

"In more ways than one," David added. "From where I stand, she's a sitting target for a bunch of sleazy jerks as long as she stays there."

Lauren frowned. "So where do you want me to go, oh Wise One? I haven't found an apartment yet, and even when I do, I'm sure they can track me down. There are such things as public records and sickos with not enough to do but follow me around."

"Oh, I have a solution, all right." Mischief colored his grin. "It's the best place for you, and I doubt even you could object."

Grandma Dottie wagged a finger at David. "You'd better not be up to your goofy practical jokes again."

"Yeah, Davey boy. Where are you gonna . . . um . . ." Bea floundered for a word. Then she smirked. "Got it! Where you gonna *stash* her?"

David rolled his eyes then met Lauren's gaze. "Unless you have a better idea, and it would have to be a safe place — safe in my opinion — you're about to move in with my grandmother."

Grandma Dottie beamed. "Ooooh, I like that!"

Lauren at first wanted to object, mostly on principle. But then she thought of Mark. She also looked at David's grandmother, and the affection she'd begun to feel for the older woman urged her to accept, even if it felt like a surrender of her independence.

"I don't have an alternative," she said. "And if she's willing to take us in, then I'm fine with that plan."

"Oh, yeah!" Bea crowed. "I like it. I'm all for it." She turned to Lauren and Grandma Dottie. "You girls ready? We gotta get ready."

Lauren frowned. "Ready for what?"

"Yes, Bea," David added. "What are you up to now?"

"Oh, nothing much. You know. Girls just wanna have fun."

He rolled his eyes again.

Grandma Dottie snorted.

Lauren didn't even try to squelch her laugh.

Bea went on. "Let's go, ladies. Pajama party time!"

Lauren turned to David, but took pity on the guy. He, not she, was the one who'd really lost control of the situation.

"Sure thing, Bea," she said. "Let's go pack our jammies."

ELEVEN

Lauren hadn't laughed so much in years. While David and Walker's routine had only irritated her, Grandma Dottie and Bea Woodward were her very own pair of Golden Girls.

They were much more than a comedy team, though. After the police took Theodosius away, the two women and David followed Lauren to the PD. There they went through Chinese fire drill−type stealthy maneuvers with the three vehicles. In the end, the elderly women drove home with Lauren, while David took Grandma Dottie's purple Hummer to her house. All this in the hope that Theodosius's and Aloysius's pals wouldn't catch on to Lauren's change of address. David had plans for retrieving the women after he picked up Mark at school.

The senior citizens helped Lauren pack enough to keep her and Mark going for a couple of days. They also agreed to return in the morning and for as many days as it took to box the rest of her belongings, get the furniture ready for David and his motley crew of movers, and then get the home in spiffy open house condition.

Packing with the seniors was an experience in itself. Very little got past them without comment.

"Love this bedroom set, Lauren," Bea said. "But you're going to have to find yourself a new place with ten-foot ceilings."

Lauren looked at her late parents' tall, four-poster bed. "I could always sell it."

Grandma Dottie looked from the bed to Lauren. "This furniture means a great deal to you, doesn't it?"

"It was my parents'."

"Well, then I've just got myself a borrowed bedroom set. That is, until you find a home that'll do it justice."

"Boooooooring!" Bea chimed in. "What you mean, Dot, is that you scored a load of freebies until Lauren lands a wicked good pad."

"Good one," Grandma Dottie said with a grin.

Lauren chuckled, but then said, "I can't impose on you like that. Besides, these pieces are huge. I'm sure you have a houseful of furniture already."

"And who says we can't have Walker and Davey shove my stuff aside and store yours with it until you can use it again?"

"Like the way you think, Dot," Bea said. "And Lauren, I rattle around my pad all by myself. I can stash an awesome lot of loot for you, too."

A knot formed in Lauren's throat at the generosity of the two women. "Thanks," she murmured. Then the phone rang. "Di-Stefano residence."

"Hello, Lauren. It's Don D'Amato. How are you doing? I haven't seen you since Ric's funeral, and I know how hard his death hit you."

If he only knew! "I'm doing well. How's your family?"

"Bella's in New York giving my credit cards a Christmas workout, and the boys keep me running every night with basketball practices and games. How's Mark?"

"He misses Ric, but other than that, he's happy and healthy."

"I don't blame the little guy. I'm a whole lot older, and I miss Ric, too." He paused, and Lauren wondered why this man, Ric's friend from high school, had called. She didn't ask, but instead chose to wait for him to speak.

Then he went on. "I have a favor to ask."

"How can I help you?"

"You know Ric and I are longtime members of our Fancy Club."

"Of course."

"Well, I'd like to use pieces of Ric's costume for the parade. It's the quickest and most cost-efficient plan, since I don't have my costume ready. If you'll remember, I spent most of the year prosecuting that terror suspect."

Lauren remembered the high-profile case. "Sure, Don. That makes sense. If what I've heard is true, the costumes take an eternity to make and cost a fortune. There's no reason not to use what Ric already paid for."

"Thanks. You're a lifesaver."

Lauren tried to dismiss his lavish compliment, but he wouldn't hear of it. "Better listen to me, an officer of the court! You're saving my bacon, and I appreciate it."

"Okay, okay. But what do you want to use? How would I find it? Is it here? I don't know if he'd brought the whole thing home yet."

"You're right. What I need is the top. My headdress is almost done, and I picked up the pants three weeks ago."

"That doesn't help me, you know. How about you come and meet me here? You can dig through the plastic bags in the back of his closet."

"See? I told you you're a lifesaver. And you doubted me!"

They arranged for Don to come by the next day after Lauren dropped off Mark at school. He had a late-morning hearing in court, and could come early.

Only when she hung up, did she notice her two elderly companions. Bea and Grandma Dottie were staring at her as if she'd suddenly morphed into a green-with-orange-polka-dot-skinned alien whose several heads contained thoughts the women couldn't fathom.

"Please," Bea said. "Please, please, *please* tell me you're not part of that Mummer crowd."

Lauren frowned. "My brother was, but I'm not. What's wrong with the Mummers?"

The two friends traded meaningful looks.

Grandma Dottie came over and led Lauren to the bed. When they'd both sat down, she said, "How much do you know about your brother's hobby?"

"I only watch the parades. I don't know anything more."

Bea nodded, a serious look on her face, and took a seat on the overstuffed armchair by the window.

David's grandmother patted the hand she

174

still held. "The parades are fun, aren't they?"

"I love the music," Lauren answered. "And the costumes are so outrageous, you can't help but laugh."

"That's what makes it so popular," Bea added. "But . . ."

"But there's a dark underside to the whole thing." Grandma Dottie laid her hands on Lauren's shoulders. "I'm not saying your brother was involved with that part, but there are some who join the brigades and clubs because of their interest in paganism."

"Paganism?" Lauren's voice turned squeaky with horror. "I hope he didn't get sucked into that neo-pagan culture. But I don't get the connection."

"From what I understand," Grandma Dottie continued, "the whole Mummer thing goes back to pagan times, and has its roots in those traditions. I've heard some of the clubs are involved in modern witchcraft stuff. They believe in that whole goddess worship deal, perform spells, and are more like a coven than a social organization of folks who like to play dress up big-time."

As if she hadn't been under enough stress already! "All I can say is that I hope and pray Ric wasn't into that lifestyle. But the truth is that since he graduated high school,

I had little contact with him. Even after I moved in, he traveled constantly, and when he came home, he spent almost all his time with his fellow Mummers."

Again, the older women exchanged looks. "For your sake, and that of the boy," Bea said, all humor gone from her voice, "I hope he wasn't involved. If that's the case, it'll be tough to deal with it, and even tougher to explain to Mark at the right time. But all the time you say your brother spent with fellow Mummers, when he was a traveling man in the first place . . ."

"That does sound suspicious," Grandma Dottie added.

Lauren sighed. "I'm afraid that as time goes by, it becomes clearer that I hardly knew Ric. So anything's possible."

Bea gave an encompassing wave. "Ever come across any weird knives or chalices or funny clothes — robes and that kind of thing?"

Just the thought gave Lauren the creeps. "Other than parts of Ric's New Year's Day costumes, no. Not really."

"Then maybe he wasn't." David's grandmother injected her words with what seemed to Lauren much too much cheer.

"Maybe," Bea ventured, "while we pack up we'll find something to tell us one way or the other."

Lauren thought of the dozens of boxes in Ric's room. They'd revealed how little she knew about a major part of her late brother's life. Then, as she'd told Don, there were the garment bags in the back of Ric's closet. Since she'd known they contained the gaudy outfits, she hadn't bothered to go through them. Maybe she should. The costumes might reveal something.

On the other hand, maybe his home office with its overflowing bookshelves would be where she would find a clue.

"What's on your mind?" Grandma Dottie asked.

Lauren stood. "That we have a lot of stuff to sort. It might speak volumes about Ric."

David's grandmother slapped her thighs and rose, as well. "Ladies, it seems that the best course of action is for us to stuff the bags with what Lauren and Mark will need most, get us a good night's sleep, and come back, ready to tackle who knows what tomorrow morning."

"And maybe I can get something out of Don when he comes by."

Her two companions swapped silent visual messages for a third time.

Bea shook her head. "Don't count on it, dear. This kind of thing needs the shadow of secrecy. If this Don fellow is a pagan, well, he's going to be very, very good at keeping it to himself. You said he's a lawyer."

"That makes sense," Lauren said. "Especially since he's a prosecutor. The D.A.'s office might be uncomfortable with someone in his position involved in that alternative lifestyle."

"There's the matter of credibility for them to consider," Grandma Dottie added.

Lauren wasn't ready to give up. "All I can do is try."

She prayed for God to bless her with extra measures of wisdom, discernment and peace as she went forward. She was going to need all the help He could give.

Especially since her anger grew with each new revelation. Every day that went by, she felt more betrayed by the brother she'd loved. If Ric could so easily betray her, who else could she not trust?

Only the Lord knew.

"You did *what?*" David bellowed later that evening at Grandma Dottie's home. "Do you have a death wish?"

Lauren glared. "Of course not. But this is Don, Ric's best friend. I've known him forever. He wouldn't hurt me."

"Sure, sure. Of course, he wouldn't. Just

like Ric's turned out to be such a stand-up guy, right?"

She had no answer to that. She'd thought she'd known Ric. Turns out, she hadn't. And Don's loyalty had always been with Ric. So if the two were fellow neo-pagans, who knew what Don might do?

Then she had a thought. "Would you rather I have refused his request? Don't you think if he was ready to hurt me to get what he wanted, a refusal would have made him more likely to go that route?"

"You could be right, but I still don't like it. Last time I left you and someone came calling, your windows faced an untimely end."

"You can't wrap me in cotton, David. I know you take your job seriously, and that you want to keep Mark and me safe, but nothing on earth can stop evil. Those who refuse to live according to God's law are the only ones who can repent and turn from evil to righteousness. I don't think Aloysius or Theodosius are ready to repent, do you?"

"That's why I don't think you should have contact with anyone I haven't checked out."

"Then do it. Check out Don D'Amato. He's a prosecutor with the D.A.'s office. I'd think he's clean, wouldn't you?"

He shrugged. "Since we've suspected a

179

mole in our office, I can see anyone any-where turning."

"Cynical, aren't you?"

"I get paid to be cynical."

"If it makes you feel better, I won't be there alone. I'll have the daunting duo with me. There's safety in numbers, remember?"

He slapped his forehead. "You're betting your life on my grandmother and her moving-violation-queen pal?"

Lauren chuckled. "No. I'm putting my life in God's hands. They'll just be along for the ride."

"I'm not feeling reassured."

"That's because life's a walk of faith. I can't offer you any more assurance than that I trust God implicitly."

"You'll have to hang on to that trust. You and the daunting duo. I'll be watching from a nearby spot, but there's a lot that can go down before I can get to you."

"Then if it'll make you feel better, join us. We can use another pair of hands to pack up Ric's thousands of books."

He used his upturned hands like the bowls of a scale. "Surveillance from afar . . . pack-ing dusty books. Surveillance outside . . . packing inside. Neither one's an attractive choice."

"Neither is being watched 24-7. So what'll

it be, Special Agent Latham?"

He gave her an unexpected grin. "Hey, I've finally got you figured out. You really don't like what I just said. And I know it because you backtracked to the Mr. Latham thing again. The rest of the time, you call me David."

"How perceptive. Now, if you would please put those powers of perception to use, you'll realize I'm pooped. I need sleep."

He waved her along. "Good night. I'll let you in on my choice in the morning."

"I won't wait with bated breath."

"Good idea. I need you live and kicking."

"You're such a flatterer, you. I'm sure the ladies flock to your awe-inspiring charm."

"Hah!" Grandma Dottie said from the doorway to the room she'd given Lauren. "He's been striking zero on the romance front for a long time. I doubt he's had a date in years."

Lauren chuckled, laughed when she caught David's blush and the glare he shot his outspoken grandmother.

"Never let it be said David Latham doesn't know when it's time to split. But I won't go far. Call me if you need anything. You hear me, Gram?"

"I'm not deaf, Davey."

"Lauren?"

"I've yet to be fitted for a hearing aid."

He snorted, turned and headed for the hall.

"Whoa!" Bea blocked his exit. "You forgot me, kiddo. Or am I supposed to be the one who gets whacked?"

David looked baffled. "Huh?"

"Well, duh! You didn't ask me if I'd heard. You're falling down on your job. I'm a potential victim, too."

"Don't look so happy about it, Bea." His face took on the lines of hewn rock, while his voice sounded just as unyielding. "This isn't a movie, a game or one of your and Gram's excellent adventures."

"No, Davey. This is real," the gray-haired senior said. "It's a matter of life and death. But if we don't lighten up, we're likely to see things as if we had blinders. Tunnel vision can make for fatal mistakes."

He drew in a harsh breath. To Lauren, it looked as though his face lost a good measure of its normal color. He started down the hallway.

Over his shoulder, he called back, "Just pray."

Then he was gone.

Moments later, the three women got on their knees to do as he'd said.

■ ■ ■ ■

In the morning, Lauren assigned the kitchen and all its paraphernalia to Bea. Grandma Dottie got Mark's room. Lauren headed for Ric's office and the million books stuffed in the floor-to-ceiling shelves.

Two hours and fourteen packed book boxes later, Lauren made an unhappy discovery. More than one, actually.

Modern Witchcraft. Casting the Effective Spell. Goddess Worship. And there were more, many more such titles. A shudder of revulsion shook her, and she began to hurl the books to the floor from where she stood on top of the library ladder. They made a satisfying *thunk* when they hit the hardwood boards.

Moments later, Grandma Dottie and Bea ran into the room.

"Lauren!" Bea called. "Are you okay?"

Grandma Dottie watched openmouthed as Lauren heaved two more of the offending missiles floorward. "*What* is wrong with you? I never thought I'd see a teacher do that to a bunch of books."

Lauren clenched her fists at her sides. "Just read the titles, ladies. I think you'll support my efforts, maybe even join me."

183

The women looked from Lauren on the ladder to the books she'd hurled to the floor. Then Bea trotted to the nearest tome, picked it up, checked out the spine and threw it back down with as much *oomph* as Lauren had used.

"You get it now, don't you?" she asked.

Bea nodded. "Let me help you. I'll bet you want this filth out of your home as soon as possible."

"But it's not my home," Lauren said. "It belonged to Ric. As did all the records of crooks' dirty business deals. As did all these books."

"So it turned out to be true," Grandma Dottie murmured.

"Too true," Lauren countered. "I'm just glad our father went home to the Lord well before Ric turned his back on all we were raised to hold dear."

"Before he turned from the faith," Bea added.

Lauren nodded. "Before he betrayed not just his earthly father and his sister. Before he betrayed Almighty God."

TWELVE

To say she didn't get a good night's sleep would be a massive understatement. Lauren lay on the bed in the elegant bedroom and stared at the ceiling with its gorgeous rose-embellished Capodimonte chandelier. When she couldn't stand to admire the bits and pieces of it any longer, she studied the intricate carving on the mahogany dresser illuminated by the glow of the streetlight outside. By the time she got tired of switching between the two, she closed her eyes, and tried to make herself fall asleep.

But fast flashes of memory burst a medley of images to life behind her eyelids. Those flashes showed first the brother of her childhood, then the caricature in sequins he later became. She saw the beautiful home she cared for over the last three years turn into an ugly trap where vicious violence targeted her. A quiet walk home after she picked up a sleepy Mark from a friend's home — she'd stayed longer than planned to chat with a group of mothers at a parents' event at school — changed into a failed murder attempt.

She no longer could identify normal. She couldn't even tell real from surreal. Her world now looked like nothing more than a space filled with smoke and lined with mirrors that turned all she'd ever known into a foggy alternate universe.

And then the questions. Who were Aloysius and Theodosius?

For that matter, who had Ric really been?

Would Don turn out to be another Jekyll and Hyde guy?

Who had really been behind the wheel of that Lexus?

And who were the criminals whose coffers Ric helped fill? Had he worked for the mob, as she'd come to fear? Or had he been part of that underworld, as David and Walker suspected?

Beyond all the questions from the past that now colored her present, a shaky future spread out before her. How would she provide for Mark? Even more important, would she be able to protect him, keep him safe?

As the hours crawled by, Lauren found it harder and harder to even try to relax. The betrayal she'd begun to feel as she lifted the unattractive layers from her late brother's life filled her with anger again, hotter and more focused now. How could he have done this?

How could a father indulge in illegal activities? Didn't he know it would sooner or later taint his little boy? And Lauren knew Ric had loved Mark.

Sure, hers was a naive — maybe even innocent — thought, but she'd never imagined her brother could be anything but innocent of illegal activity.

The whole situation was wrong. Just plain *wrong.* And she was now stuck picking up the pieces. How could she be expected to move forward? How could she begin to plan for tomorrow when she couldn't even see today for all the junk from yesterday Ric had left behind?

By the time dawn broke, Lauren's anger felt more like rage. And betrayal burned in her gut.

Then, too, David's idiotic comment about how meek, mild and wimpy he'd thought she was didn't help matters any. When did self-control, good manners and old-fashioned politeness translate into wimpy, drippy and bland?

Boy, did she have a surprise for David

Latham.

Instead of her more typical nice slacks, tailored shirts and lightweight wool sweaters, Lauren pulled on a pair of comfortable old work jeans, a black turtleneck top, and a fire-engine-red sweatshirt. She swept her long mane of curls into a high ponytail, and contrary to her usual subtle makeup, a slick of true red lipstick gave her the courage to sail forward into the day.

But nothing served to stanch her anger.

Bea arrived, Grandma Dottie and Lauren did their shell-game routine in the hope that anyone watching the Latham home didn't realize Lauren had moved there, and then the three women left for the DiStefano home in the purple Hummer. Maybe she would look into driving one of those monsters after all. Then the David Lathams of the world wouldn't think her some kind of sappy, shrinking violet.

If she ever had the kind of money a Hummer commanded.

At the house, each went back to the job she'd started the day before. Lauren went straight to Ric's office and finished the labels for the last few boxes of books. When she stuck the last one in place, she felt a swell of satisfaction. Earlier, she'd set aside the volumes she wanted to keep, and then arranged to donate the rest to the public library. All she needed now was David, Walker and their team of movers to cart the boxes to the waiting librarians.

Even though it was only midmorning, and she still had a whole day ahead of her, she felt drained. The natural break in the packing marathon gave her the opportunity to relax for a few minutes. The comfortable wingback leather chairs on either side of the tall window beckoned and, with a heartfelt sigh, she collapsed into one.

David's deep voice woke her up. "Anybody come by yet, Gram?"

Lauren dragged herself out of the chair and went in search of her very own FBI shadow. No matter how many times she told herself to keep a lid on her resentment, to pray, turn her feelings over to the Lord, she didn't succeed.

"Did you change your mind about sticking to us like a hungry flea on a stray mutt?"

"I followed the Hummer earlier, but I got a call, had to run in to the office, and just got back."

"As far as I know, it's only been the three of us here. But I did fall asleep for a little while."

"Good — on both counts," he said. "Where can I hide while you and the Mummer go through your brother's costumes?"

Was he serious? "Hide? You're not exactly pocket-size, David. The costumes are in the closet, so that's out. You can't crawl under the bed since you dismantled that. The door doesn't offer enough space behind it, and I can't imagine any other corner where I might squirrel you away."

His jaw set like concrete. "You'd better get busy and find one. There's no way I'm leaving you at the mercy of this guy."

Lauren narrowed her gaze. "Your agent friend must have come upon a red flag when he investigated Don. What is it?"

He shoved his hands in his pockets, looked away from her. "He's not managed to get a whole lot of his defendants convicted. A bunch of jerks who should be behind bars are still walking Philly's streets."

"And so you've decided Don's a crook." She blew a stray curl off her forehead. "Ever think the jerks had high-power lawyers to get them off?"

"Every single one?"

"It could happen."

"So could the arrival of Martians for dinner, but I don't think we have to add to the soup pot just yet."

Again, exhaustion drained Lauren. "Look, if you're done badgering me, why don't you go find yourself a hole to crawl into so you can spy on Don and me when he gets here?"

He blinked.

"Oh, I see. You miss the wimp you thought I was." She grinned. "Let me flash you a news break. It's not too smart to confuse manners with wishy-washiness. I'm not a doormat, and I'm tired of your high-handed bossiness."

"Just remember, my high-handed bossiness saved your hide on that street that night. Your sudden boldness won't get you far when you come up against the working end of a gun."

Lauren glared. "Okay. I hear you. I'll keep that in mind. And now, since I didn't sleep at all last night, I'm going to take a nap. Enjoy your rat hole, Mr. Latham."

Never had it felt better to crawl into her bed. Sleep came blessedly fast.

Rat hole? She saw him as a rodent?

David couldn't believe the change in Lauren. Or had he misread her? Since this was the second time the thought crossed his mind, he probably had.

"Great."

Now he'd also alienated her. And that bothered him. From the start, Lauren had struck him as a dangerous woman. Not violent, not crooked, not a physical threat, but feminine, smart, very pretty, devoted to her nephew and full of love for the Lord.

Everything a man could want in a woman.

And he no longer could force out his usual, "Not this man."

Something about this sassier version of his current assignment appealed to him in an even more powerful way. He felt pretty sure she could — and would — face off against him toe-to-toe. Something told him she was going to challenge him, give him a run for his money, in more ways than one.

But he couldn't afford to explore any of those possibilities. Not only was she a job — he still had to protect her — but he also wasn't ready to surrender his freedom. He had to remember his marriage-phobia, his determination to remain single for life, to stay the consummate bachelor. The single life allowed him to pursue the career he loved without a load of guilt about the effect it might have on a wife and family.

To distract himself from risky thoughts, David went in search of the daunting duo, as Lauren had begun to call his grandmother and Bea. They were daunting, all right. Scary, to be precise.

He found them knee-deep in packaging supplies. "What are you up to?" he asked when an airborne Styrofoam peanut hit him on the nose.

"What's it look like we're up to, Davey?" Gram shook her head. "Sometimes I have to wonder about you."

"That's not what I meant. I know you're here helping Lauren pack, but why are you making like a pair of dandelions in a field of packing peanuts? What'd you break?"

Bea rolled her eyes and tsk-tsked. "Didn't you listen when I told you the other night? Girls just wanna have fun."

"So you flung a million peanuts all over the place for no reason — ah! Sorry. That's right. You tossed peanuts for the fun of it. So who gets to have fun picking them up?"

Maybe it was time to move them into an assisted living facility; they needed keepers. But knowing his grandmother, it'd be one of those she'd-like-to-see-him-try kind of deals.

"Lighten up, Davey," his grandmother said. "Don't work so hard to give yourself a stroke or heart attack. Of course we didn't just fling peanuts all over the place. They were in big plastic bags. We had us a doozy of a peanut-pillow fight."

"I get it. Tossing peanuts — bad. Explosive peanut-pillow fights — good."

Before she had a chance to concoct a

zingy comeback to that, he was saved by the doorbell.

Swell. He'd let a pair of geriatric adolescents distract him from his job. "Give me a minute to find somewhere to hide. This has to be that lawyer friend of Lauren's brother, and I want to keep an eye on him while he's here with her."

Bea's gray eyes danced with mischief. "Oooooh! Spy duty. *Fun!*"

"Behave!" he said as he ran for cover. And began to pray. He had no illusions about Bea and Gram. Who knew what they'd come up with next? Only the Lord could keep up with those two.

Minutes later, he hit paydirt . . . of sorts. The things he did for his job! Just a foot beyond Ric's bedroom door he found the attic access panel in the hall ceiling. He pulled it down, gave the Lord thanks for the attached ladder, climbed up, dragged the ladder back into place, but didn't close the trapdoor all the way. He hoped Don D'Amato had a voice that carried well.

Before long, he heard footsteps on the landing. He was glad this gig was getting started. A killer draft ran through the attic, cobwebs draped his face, and he wasn't sure it wasn't a rodent he'd heard in the far corner of an eave.

Not the most splendid circumstances to find himself in. Especially since he had to practically sit on the trapdoor to hear the conversation below.

The chitchat about the D'Amato offspring didn't interest him; the young kids weren't involved in the investigation. Neither did Mrs. D'Amato's shopping extravagances have any bearing on his case. He did wonder, though, how she could afford those lavish shopping sprees on her prosecutor husband's salary.

Then things got interesting.

"That's the one," D'Amato said. "Wow! Paulie outdid himself this year. That's amazing workmanship."

Lauren chuckled. "If you're the sequin-and-glass-bead kind."

"Yeah, well, I'm usually the wool gabardine or summer linen kind, but everything changes when it comes to Mummery."

Her response came after a heartbeat of silence. "So I hear." After a longer pause she asked, "What's the appeal, Don? I've never understood."

"I'm not sure I understand it myself. Other than the masquerade's a lot of fun, and you make some pretty tight friendships with the other guys in your club."

"A male-bonding thing with a party-dress

moment."

"There's more to it than that, but I . . . ah . . . I guess I don't know how to put it into words."

"For a guy who makes his living talking to juries, you should be able to give it a stab," she said, her words full of humor.

Maybe his inability to put things into words was D'Amato's problem, the reason he lost all but a handful of his cases. But David didn't really think so.

D'Amato cleared his throat. "Ah . . . didn't you ask Ric any of these questions? Didn't he tell you all about it?"

"When did I have a chance to carry on any kind of conversation with him, Don?" Lauren's voice took on that bit of a nip that always surprised him. "You know how much he traveled. And when he came home to Philly, Ric spent more time with you and the 'guys' from the club than he did here."

David heard a zipper opened. Then D'Amato said, "Look at this one! Remember that year? I really liked the yellow and red color scheme, didn't you?"

"It was nice," Lauren answered. "You do agree that Ric spent more time with you than here with Mark and me?"

D'Amato cleared his throat. "It takes a ton of time to prepare for a parade, you know. We have to choose music, practice the lineup, decide how we're going to better show off that year's theme, and there's always the design, construction, fittings, adjustments to the costumes. It may look like fun to those on the side of the road, but there's a lot of work and detail involved in getting that parade up the street."

David thought D'Amato did protest too much.

"I get it." Sarcasm sounded good on Lauren's voice.

Hangers scraped against a closet rod, and the sound muffled anything D'Amato might have said — not that David thought the visitor actually said a word. He'd begun to suspect that Ric's pal had as secret a double life as Lauren's brother had.

"How about you tell me about that 'more' you said there was to Mummery?"

"There's really not a whole lot to tell. It's kind of intangible. You know, a guy thing."

"But that's just it. I *don't* know anything about guy stuff. Why don't you help me understand? You can start by telling me about the Mummers' club experience."

"Oh, would you look at the time! I have to be at the court in fifteen minutes, and I still have morning traffic to survive. I'm afraid I have to go —"

"Come on. Don't be such a tease, Don."

David tensed up. Lauren was pushing. He didn't want her to spook D'Amato. But then she surprised him — again.

"Just give me a clue here," she said with a sad little quiver in her voice. "I miss Ric so much. It would really help me if I knew a little more of what made him who he was."

D'Amato didn't answer. Then David heard heavy footsteps on the landing. He didn't want to miss Ric DiStefano's friend's spiel on the whole Mummery experience, since he'd begun to think it might have something to do with all that had happened.

He leaned forward, lowered his head close to the opening.

D'Amato spoke. "It's all about family and heritage." His voice grew fainter as they went toward the stairs.

David pressed his ear to the cracked-open trapdoor.

". . . men passing down the traditions they learned from their elders, all the way back generations —"

CRAAAASH!

David's dramatic entrance put an end to anything more DiStefano's pal might have said. It also put a dent in his skull, a bruise on his right knee, a pain in his butt and a blush on his cheeks.

D'Amato stumbled.

Lauren groaned.

David lay like an upside-down turtle, only he couldn't possibly be half as cute. He gave the two who stood over him, mouths agape, a sheepish grin. "Hi."

"Who's he?" D'Amato asked.

For a moment, Lauren looked panicked. Then she winked at David, and faced her guest. "One of the movers. He must have realized there's stuff in the attic, but look how clumsy he is. I'm going to have to call and report him."

D'Amato didn't seem ready to buy her explanation, but she didn't seem to care. She shot David a mischievous look.

"It looks like that saying's really true," she continued. "Good help's hard to find these days."

With a final, pointed look at David, D'Amato took the first step down. "Depends on the kind of help you're looking for, Lauren. Beats me what you're up to, but I can tell you I don't want to play."

She, however, played her response just right. "Don!" she cried with just enough shock, hurt, dismay and defensiveness. "How can you say that? I'm not playing at anything. What do you mean by that comment?"

"Only that I know I've seen that 'mover' somewhere before. Can't quite place him right now — it's not usual to see a guy drop flat on his back from above — but I have a pretty decent memory. Sooner or later I'll figure it out. Then I'll know exactly what's going on."

He didn't add any more after that, but David didn't need any more. He knew where D'Amato was going with his words, his threat. Did Lauren?

A glance her way surprised him again. A momentary flicker of what looked like fear crossed her face, but then she squared her shoulders and followed D'Amato down the stairs.

"Maybe, Don," she said in a calm, even voice, "I'll know what's going on then, too."

Admiration filled David. D'Amato had challenged Lauren. But to his surprise, she'd countered with a challenge of her own.

She was a gutsy lady.

He was glad he'd met her.

Now, he just had to make sure she lived long enough.

He was too much of a coward, tough, guarded warrior that he liked to think he was, to consider what exactly he wanted her to live long enough for.

But God knew. And that was enough for

David to get to his feet and follow Lauren downstairs. Scarier, though, was the thought that he might be ready to follow her anywhere, anytime, all the time.

Heaven help him, because he suspected he'd become powerless to do otherwise. Thanks to a gentle, smart, daring woman, he felt smaller than that other David must have felt when he squared off against Goliath all those centuries ago.

THIRTEEN

After David returned to his bland, nondescript spymobile outside and the three women finished their soup and sandwiches, Lauren found the life insurance payout in that day's mail.

Check in hand, she called the money-men and agreed to meet them at one-thirty. She dressed in something adequate, slipped the check in her handbag and did her surreptitious departure routine again.

On the Hummer ride to Ric's investment counselor's office, Grandma Dottie tacked with no logic the butchered lyrics from favorite musicals, nursery rhymes, folk songs and old rock 'n' roll to random tunes. The weird serenade boomed around the inside of the erstwhile military vehicle in a voice that could obliterate decibel meters.

By the time David's grandmother started out "On Top of Old Smokey" then ventured that "If She'd Had a Hammer" the "Eensy

Weensy Spider" wouldn't have gone up the spout, Lauren had counted to a thousand by sevens. Endurance, appreciation and mercy sometimes took more to produce than the average woman had on hand.

She never thought she'd run toward imminent bankruptcy and homelessness, but that's what she did when she leaped from the Hummer and rushed into the building to pay off Ric's debts.

It took a depressingly short time to use up almost a million dollars. But the relief Lauren felt after she'd eliminated the burden of Ric's unpaid accounts was worth every penny she spent.

She only wished the money could have stretched to cover the mortgage. On the other hand, she had to admit that hanging with Grandma Dottie was an experience, the kind of fun she and Mark needed to get past the worst of the grief.

She climbed back into the Hummer. "Okay, Grandma Dottie. That's done."

"Feel better?"

"It's amazing how easy it is to have a million dollars slip through your fingers."

"It wasn't a loss, honey, but rather a gain. Peace of mind is worth all that and more."

"I agree. And it's funny you should mention peace of mind. There's one more stop I need to make before we can go home."

"Where's that?"

"Since I'm practically destitute, I have to find myself a job. The principal at the school where I used to teach said I would always have a job there. I'd like to go see what's possible now."

"You're not destitute as long as you're with me."

"Oh, I can't live off you."

"You're not living off me. You're providing me with valuable treasures. I was lonely, and you brought me company. I miss my children and grandchildren now that they're all adults. Mark brings out the child in me again. I can't even begin to put a value on all that."

The lump in Lauren's throat made it impossible to answer right away. When she wiped the tear from her cheek and swallowed hard, she said, "That's the sweetest thing anyone's ever said to me, and you bless Mark and me more than you'll know. That doesn't mean that I can sponge off you. I'm not comfortable without income, no matter how great your generosity."

For a moment, she thought David's grandmother was about to object. But then Dorothea Stevens Latham surprised her again.

She laughed!

"I didn't think anything I said was all that funny."

"It wasn't. Sorry." Grandma Dottie started up the powerful engine. "I just think you're the best thing that's happened to my grandson in his entire life. Let's hope he's smart enough to see it."

What did a woman say to that?

"Um . . . the school's all the way across town." She gave directions, Grandma Dottie drove — and sang — and Lauren prepared herself for the ordeal ahead. She'd never liked job interviews, and this one would probably be more uncomfortable than most.

But there was no way around it. And in a short quarter hour, they arrived at the school.

"Thanks," she told Grandma Dottie.

"I'm praying for you, honey. For the Father's will."

The knot returned to her throat, but she had to fight the emotional reaction. She had to speak, and do so well. Mark's future depended on her success today.

With a flutter in her middle, she entered the building where she'd spent so many happy days.

"Lauren!"

When she turned, Sara Beth Lawton, the

205

school's latest and best secretary, threw her arms around her neck and held on tight. This time, Lauren couldn't stop the tears.

"I've missed you so much," the slender brunette said. "I know you've been busy with your little nephew and that huge house, but maybe we can get together for lunch sometime. You have to come out from hiding every once in a while, you know."

"I haven't been hiding, Sara Beth. I've been busy, just like you said."

"Tell you what, girl. I'm going to call you and drag you out to some fun place to eat."

She'd need money to buy herself that meal. "Is Audrey in her office? Do you know if she'd have a few minutes to spare for me?"

"Oh, she's in, and if she hears you've been here and haven't popped in to see her . . . oh, girl! I wouldn't want to be you then."

Lauren chuckled. "She's not that bad, you nut. Now go see if she's free. Please."

Sara Beth went back to her desk, punched a button on her phone then spoke quietly into the speaker. To Lauren's surprise, instead of the pleasure she'd hoped to hear in her former — and hopefully future — boss's voice, she heard a pause. Then Audrey spoke.

"I'll be right there."

Lauren heard the click-click of tall heels,

and then the door behind Sara Beth's desk opened. Although Audrey wore her usual bright smile, something about it struck Lauren as forced.

"How are you?" Audrey asked.

"Very busy."

Lauren's stomach clenched at the woman's brief nod. "Please come in, take a chair."

Something was wrong, terribly, terribly wrong. This was the woman who not so long ago insisted she'd always want Lauren back as a teacher, administrative staff member, even lunchroom director, if that was the only way to get her under contract again. Now, Lauren felt as though Audrey would rather entertain a hive of enraged bees than spend time with her.

Where was Grandma Dottie and the comfort she offered when Lauren most needed her? Oh, that's right. Grandma Dottie was praying. That gave her the strength to proceed.

"How're the children?" she asked, hoping for common ground.

Audrey smiled. "Wonderful, as always. Wonderfully charming, wonderfully challenging, wonderfully gifted and even wonderfully frustrating."

"I miss them," Lauren said. She sent a

silent prayer heavenward, and then continued. "Which is what brings me here. I'm hoping I can take you up on your offer. Do you have any openings I could fill? My brother died, left us in a terrible financial situation, and I need to earn a living —"

"Let me stop you right there." Audrey removed the delicate, rimless glasses and rubbed the spot where they'd lain on the bridge of her nose. "This is going to be one of the hardest things I've had to do in my twenty-three-year career. You were one of the finest educators we ever employed. And I do have a vacancy. Darlene Sutton goes on maternity leave as of December twenty-second. . . ."

Fear, crushing disappointment and anger crashed and burned in Lauren's gut. "I'd like to know the *but,* Audrey."

The school principal stood behind her desk. "But we have to put the children's welfare before everything else. And I can't do that if I bring you back to the school."

That brought Lauren to her feet. "Are you saying I'd hurt the children? Audrey! Have you lost your mind? It's me. Lauren DiStefano. I would never harm a child —"

"Not willingly. That I know beyond a shadow of a doubt. But your presence here could lead parents to withdraw students,

208

and even lawsuits are possible."

Lauren stared, listened and heard, but couldn't grasp what was happening. The sinking sensation from her old boss's words left her off-kilter, dizzy even. Nothing made sense.

"Why would anyone sue because of me? I've never hurt anyone — I don't even have a speeding or parking ticket in my past. I don't understand. Please explain what's happened?"

Audrey drew a deep breath. "Actually, you're the one who needs to explain. All I know is that about a week ago, an agent with the Organized Crime Division of the FBI came by with a million questions about you. He made it perfectly clear that you're under investigation."

"No, no! Not me. I'm not the one they're investigating. It's my brother Ric. The Securities and Exchange Commission is looking at some strange business deals he made before he died."

Pity filled the look Audrey sent her. "That may be what they told you, but trust me, Lauren. They're investigating you, too."

Anger? Oh, she'd thought she'd known anger. But now she knew she hadn't had a clue.

She saw red. "That filthy, rotten, lying,

hypocrite! 'We have to make sure you're safe.' 'We don't want anything to happen to you.' " She narrowed her eyes. "Of course, he doesn't! He wants to nail me for stuff I didn't do. He's trying to trap me!"

"Who's the hypocrite?" Audrey asked, curiosity in every line on her face.

"Oh, I'm sure you know him well by now. I've been under protective custody — supposedly. The guy who came to interrogate you has been on my heels ever since the night some idiot tried to run me over."

An idiot who looked a lot like her dead brother . . . or could it have actually been her brother behind the wheel? She no longer was certain of anything. Was Ric really dead? Was he somehow alive and still driving?

Had Ric tried to kill her?

"That's awful," Audrey said. "Are you okay?"

"Just a couple of scrapes and bruises."

"Well, thankfully it wasn't serious." She closed her eyes for a moment. Then, "But you must understand our position with all that going on. We can't hire someone the FBI's investigating."

"I can understand what scares you, but of course I don't agree, much less like it. But I won't take any more of your time."

Lauren turned, opened the door. "Just

210

wait until I get my hands on that arrogant, big-headed, pompous jerk. He's going to wish himself another assignment." She left the office, sent Sara Beth a grim, tight smile then headed out to the Hummer. "Ooooh! Grandma Dottie's not going to be too happy about the lies he's told me —"

A horrible thought brought her mutters to a screeching halt. Had he set up his own grandmother as a spy? Or, worse yet, was she even his grandmother? Could she be part of the FBI's operation?

Lauren stopped in the entrance to the school. She could see the outrageous purple Hummer right where she'd left it in the parking lot. Half of her wanted to rush out and collapse into Grandma Dottie's arms. The other half wanted to run away from the overwhelming sense that she no longer knew anything about herself, her world, or all she'd always held dear.

Her brother had betrayed her. The woman who'd promised to hire her back anytime she wanted had turned on her. The FBI agent who said he had to protect her had a totally different agenda. Her brother's lifelong best friend was hiding something. And worse yet, the woman who only minutes earlier had called her a valuable treasure could very well be as much a traitor as that weasel grandson of hers.

Desperation filled Lauren. Where could she go? Where could she turn? What was she going to do? Who could she trust?

Where was God in all of this? Had He abandoned her, too? What had she done for him to turn His back on her? She'd never felt so alone, so hopeless.

She had no one on her side.

Even the FBI had sent her a rat in agents' clothing.

Who would trust a hairless-tailed rodent with her life?

It had to be here somewhere. David yanked open drawer after drawer in his ancient, rusty-cornered metal file cabinet. He burrowed through each and every file in each and every drawer, but in the end, it didn't matter how hard he looked. The DiStefano file wasn't there.

And he knew he'd put it back in the top drawer.

He'd checked the other ones just in case he'd looked through the file another time he didn't remember, and then forgotten where he'd filed it. But it wasn't in the cabinet.

It wasn't anywhere in the shoe box he called an office.

He tore apart his desk, but had no success there, either. All the books on his shelves found their way to the floor. He found nothing under or behind them — not that he'd expected to find the file there, but he'd had to try. At the end of the frustrating endeavor, he had no choice but to accept reality.

The file was gone.

He trucked down the hall and into Eliza's office. Hers was the real deal, with enough room to turn around, and even to have someone come, sit and talk for a while in relative comfort. She didn't do a lot he could measure, but she was the Supervising Special Agent. He didn't bother to knock, since she had no one with her.

"We have a problem," he said.

Her deep green eyes became narrow, angry slits. "Yes, we certainly do. You have no concept of common courtesy. Ever hear of knocking before you barge into someone's private space?"

"Get real. This is an office, not private space." He shook his head. "You seem to forget that detail way too often."

"Just as often as you and your pals forget you're supposed to be professionals." She pointed a scarlet-tipped finger at the chair across her desk. "Take a seat and tell me what brought on this latest tantrum."

"No tantrum, Eliza. Looks like we have us a sticky-fingered office crasher."

Her eyes widened, her lips tightened, her cheeks reddened. "What exactly are you saying?"

"That someone went into my office and lifted a file. The DiStefano file."

She stared at him. It seemed to him she had trouble deciding whether she believed him or not. Then she smiled. It wasn't pleasant. "I'd be very careful with what I say, David. You don't spend a whole lot of time around here, and you could have left that file anywhere."

He snorted. "It's my current case, Eliza. I've looked at that file about a hundred times in the last ten or twelve days. I didn't leave it anywhere. I filed it alphabetically each time I put it away."

"Don't worry too much about it. I'm sure it'll turn up somewhere."

"And what do I do about my current assignment? I've made notes, recorded data, updated what was in there when you handed me that lousy excuse for a case file."

"So put together a new file. It's not such a big deal. You weren't ready to close the case, were you?"

Disgust pushed him out of his chair.

"Forget it, okay? Just forget it. I'll deal with it."

"Good. I'm glad you see it my way."

The thought of a stolen case file struck David as anything but good. He'd never lost a file in all the years he'd worked for the Bureau. He'd never lost a file period. Not in college, not at work.

Something was very wrong here. And it could affect Lauren and Mark. He wasn't ready to risk that possibility, so he went straight to J.Z.'s office. That one was even smaller than his cubicle, thanks to Eliza. When she took the job J.Z. had been offered after David's friend broke off their relationship, she'd rearranged the entire department, and her former flame wound up with the worst quarters.

But J.Z. had never complained. He dealt with the slight by ignoring it altogether and loving his brand-new wife.

Because of the room's small size, J.Z. rarely closed the door. Today was no different; however, it was even more crowded than usual. Dan Maddox lay draped like a massive amoeba all over the only chair besides J.Z.'s.

"How's it going?" Dan asked.

"Not as good as it should."

J.Z. leaned forward, his dark eyes intense.

"Care to elaborate?"

"Sure. Someone lifted the DiStefano case file from my cabinet."

Dan's slouch became a thing of the past. "Say what?"

"You heard me. Someone stole that file."

J.Z. rapped his fingers on the desktop in a tight rhythm. "I assume you tore the office apart already, right?"

"Twice."

Dan looked at J.Z. then at David again. J.Z. looked at David then back at Dan. David looked from one to the other man.

J.Z. nodded.

David closed the door.

"How's your memory?" J.Z. asked.

"Just as good as yours," David answered.

"I don't forget a thing," Dan added.

J.Z. studied the shiny new gold band on his left ring finger. "Maryanne says hi. She misses Carlie, Dan. They haven't been able to talk since she went into the witness protection program."

"Carlie's fine," Dan said. "But she does miss Maryanne. Says she wants to do girl stuff with her, and can't wait for her situation to come to an end."

David didn't need much of a translator. J.Z.'s wife had been a suspect in the murder of Carlie Papparelli's husband. At that time,

J.Z. had insisted someone at the office had turned traitor. Dan and David hadn't given his suspicion much credit, since neither man wanted to consider the possibility of a mole sabotaging their efforts.

But now, he knew someone had taken that file. And Lauren's brother had a connection to Carlie's late husband, the man many suspected Maryanne had killed back then.

"Wanna go for doughnuts?" Dan asked.

J.Z. stood, his tall, lean body taut, tense, the expression on his face dangerous. "I'm kinda hungry, now that you mention it."

"I can go for a sugar buzz." David opened the door again. "The doughnut shop down the street has decent coffee, too. I've only had three cups this morning."

Dan zipped up his black leather bomber jacket. "Then it's a deal. Let's go sink our teeth into the sweet stuff."

"The sweet stuff," David echoed.

If only they really had doughnuts in mind. A brainstorming session under these conditions had nothing sweet about it. But the solution to the puzzle would be totally sweet.

So would telling Lauren she was finally safe.

David prayed for that moment to come soon.

FOURTEEN

Awkwardness shrouded the ride home. Lauren had to give credit where credit was due. Grandma Dottie took one look at her when Lauren opened the purple passenger door, started up the engine and drove in silence.

Lauren couldn't have stood another massacred song.

But the older woman's obvious sensitivity hit Lauren in the wounded corner of her heart. Could someone who understood her emotional upheaval, who'd reached out and welcomed her and Mark, who'd said she wanted to share her wealth, home, love, with them be part of David's sneaky spy games?

She slanted a look at Grandma Dottie. Her concern showed everywhere Lauren looked, in the slight frown on her forehead, the tight line of her lips and in the white knuckles on the steering wheel. Then there were the worried little glances David's grandmother sent Lauren's way every few blocks. She couldn't ignore or discount those.

Could that be love in the nutty senior citizen's gaze? Or was it fear she might have been busted?

Either way, Lauren didn't know what to say. Not during the drive, not when they arrived at the lavish Latham mansion. She'd loved it when she learned the history of the place. Grandma Dottie had said her late husband's grandfather had built the home at the end of the nineteenth century once his law practice became established and profitable. His wife had treasured the place, choosing only the finest pieces to enhance the beautiful craftsmanship evident everywhere.

By the time Grandma Dottie and her husband inherited the home, the family fortunes, while not devastated, weren't as flush as they'd once been. The couple worked hard with their God-given talents to make the best of the inherited portfolio. The house now showed their hard work, and Grandma Dottie constantly gave the Lord thanks for how he'd blessed them through all those years.

Lauren loved the mahogany paneling in the library, the stained glass windows in the dining room and on the stair landing, the marble-and-limestone fireplace, the exquisite parquet floor and all the many details one found no matter where one looked. And while it had felt like a sanctuary from the moment she first arrived, now she had to wonder how much of a fool she'd been. Had she put herself in worse jeopardy by coming here? Had she let down her defenses too much? Could she afford to let down her guard anywhere?

Ever?

She sighed just inside the door. She couldn't leave, either. She had to make the best of the situation, if not for her, then for Mark's sake. She walked into the gorgeous living room.

"Aunt Lauren! Where you been? Monster Man took me to McDonald's after school!"

Lauren wasn't a big fan of fast food, but she didn't have the heart to rain on Mark's male-bonding parade. "Did you have fun?"

"Yeah! See? See? Lookit what I got."

He held out the small, plastic toy that came with children's meals. Lauren turned the bagged thing over in her hands. "What is it?"

His big green eyes met hers. " 'M'not sure. But it's cool! Way cool."

Wonder where he'd picked up that bit of slang? "I'm glad you like it —"

"What's wrong with my grandson?" Grandma Dottie exclaimed, her disapproval exaggerated for Mark's sake. "He fed you that stuff?"

Mark glanced over a shoulder. Then he pressed a finger to his lips. "Shh, Gramma! He loves burgers 'n fried, and we don't wanna hurt his feelings."

Lauren would like to hurt more than David's feelings, but pride in her nephew's tenderhearted nature knew no bounds. "Don't worry, Mark. David's a big boy. He can take care of himself."

The big boy's grandmother turned sharp eyes on Lauren. "Did Monster Man show you how to use that thing?" she asked. When Mark shook his head, she added, "Go ask him. He's got to be good for something other than ruining your appetite."

"He dinn'nt ruin nothing," Mark said earnestly. "I'm starving!"

"We'll see when I give you the yummy beef and potatoes I have in my roaster."

Mark took the toy and trotted from the kitchen. His "Yum!" echoed in the hallway.

"Okay, missy," Grandma Dottie said in a firm voice. "How about you give me a clue?"

Lauren had known this moment would come soon enough, but she hadn't looked forward to its arrival. Now that it was here, she wanted to run. But she'd never been a coward, and she wasn't going to start now.

"I had a nasty experience at the school. As I'm sure you've figured out, I'm still unemployed."

"I figured that out when you walked out, but my question is why?"

Time to face reality. Lauren dropped her handbag on the antique French bombé chest near the door. She then took a seat on the brocade-covered settee. Finally, she met Grandma Dottie's gaze.

"It turns out someone got there before me."

"Oh, dear. I'm so sorry they'd already filled the spot —"

"That's far from what happened." David's grandmother looked bewildered so Lauren went on to clear her confusion. "They still have a vacancy, a perfect one for me, but they feel I'm no longer fit to be around children."

"What idiot would think that?"

"Audrey Norman is no idiot, but there are idiots involved. *One* idiot has done plenty of harm."

Grandma Dottie sat on the bergère style chair across from Lauren. "This word game is unlike you, Lauren. You've been very direct since the day we met. What's wrong?

Please don't hedge anymore. I can't help if I don't know what needs to be fixed."

"Your grandson needs to be fixed."

Dorothea Stevens Latham's eyes bulged. "What did you say?"

"David isn't the sweet, innocent, decent boy you'd like to think him." That is, if she wasn't in on the betrayal, too. "He pretends to be concerned about me — Mark and me — but when he's out of my sight, he's busy casting doubt on my integrity. He paid my former boss a visit, and told her I'm under FBI investigation."

Grandma Dottie's jawline grew taut and square. "I don't understand."

"According to Audrey, I'm a suspect, but I'm not sure what I'm suspected of doing."

"David wouldn't do that. I can't believe it."

"He did, and according to Audrey, a woman who carries that kind of baggage would give the school a bad image. She even hinted that I might be a bad influence on the children."

"It's your dead brother who's under the microscope. Not you."

"That's what I thought, but it seems your hypocrite grandson has been investigating me all along —"

"I'm no hypocrite, and you're not the

223

target of my investigation. Where'd you buy yourself that paranoid idea?"

"I can't afford a shopping trip, and wouldn't spend a penny on paranoia. My former boss, who rejected me for a position I'm perfectly qualified for, all on the basis of your little visit, told me about it. You didn't seem to mince words with her."

He looked from Lauren to his grandmother and back. "I feel like an endangered species. One of those stupid insects no one's ever heard of, and could care less whether they live or die." He raked long fingers through his hair. "I don't have a clue who your former boss might be."

Lauren shook a finger at him. "Ah, ah, ah! Don't go there. Are you sure you want to add liar to hypocrite?"

"I don't lie. And I don't know your old boss. I don't know what you're talking about."

"Then explain to me why she said you stopped by, asked a ton of questions about me, and then finished it all off by telling her you were investigating me."

His jaw looked like a chunk of granite. "Beats me. But *I* did not go to your former place of employment."

Lauren crossed her arms. "Would you like me to believe Audrey lied to me? Why would she link me to an FBI probe out of the blue? Seems to me that would take a serious case of delusional creativity."

"I didn't say she's delusional," he said. "But I have never met her or spoken with her. Don't forget the SEC's involved in this case. Maybe one of their investigators —"

"Nice try, pal. But it won't fly. Whoever was there specifically mentioned the FBI."

Grandma Dottie crossed to David's side. "One question. Are you investigating Lauren? Not her brother or his business or his friends. Is she the target of your investigation?"

His cheeks went red and his eyes narrowed. "No! My assignment began after that car hit her. I recognized the last name, brought up the incident to my boss, and she assigned me to protect Lauren. The protection made sense since her brother's affairs were in question and the hit-and-run threatened her."

His voice rang with what sounded to Lauren like sincerity, but she didn't trust him. Not anymore. Not that she'd trusted him all that much from the start.

True, David Latham was an appealing man. His intensity projected the image of strong convictions, of honesty and integrity. His repeated promises of protection had lulled her into accepting his words — accepting him.

In the end, however, he turned out to be no different from her brother. The FBI no better than . . .

Maybe they were as bad as the pagan shadows behind her brother and the world of Mummers. She didn't trust any of them. Not now.

And she told him just that.

The red on his cheeks darkened. "You're letting the disappointment from that bad job interview warp your view of reality."

"On the contrary. I feel as though I'm only now seeing clearly."

"So everyone in the world is out to get you?" He shook his head. "Why? What makes you such a target? What are you hiding?"

She glared. "Nothing! You're the one who's hiding something here. You're hiding the reason for your so-called protection. What you're really doing is spying on me."

"I keep going back to my question. Why would I bother to spy on you? I don't have that much time on my hands. My job tends to consume every minute of every day."

"Beats me. You're the one with the slimy job. I'm sure you have your reasons for the wormy behavior."

"What I have is a God to answer to. I wouldn't get into that kind of fake and two-faced stuff. I'm one of the good guys. I work for the FBI —"

"Tell me another fairy tale, Agent Latham." Lauren's voice rang rich with anger and bitterness. "It's the FBI who's turned on me. I wouldn't trust you — or them — for a minute."

"That's a stupid —"

Grandma Dottie's shrill whistle cut short his latest defense. "Now then, kiddies. I'm going to run this show from here on in. No more bickering, no more blaming, no more finger-pointing. You get it?"

Lauren tore her gaze from his angry hazel eyes. "I'll do my best."

David said nothing.

"Davey?"

"What?"

"Don't do your stubborn mule impersonation," Grandma Dottie warned. "I know you too well, and I won't put up with it."

"I'm not stubborn. I'm just right."

Lauren hooted.

Grandma Dottie whistled — again.

"Why do I feel I'm dealing with kindergarteners, instead of a pair of relatively intelligent adults?" She tsk-tsked. "Work with me here. I'd like to know what's really going on, and if you continue to —" she drew a vague wave in the air "— throw these terrible tantrums, we'll never get anywhere."

Lauren tightened her arms around her middle and tapped the tip of her shoe.

David shoved his hands in his pockets and paced.

His grandmother then went on. "Has either of you remembered God lately? Remember, He's in control."

From the depths of her pain, Lauren couldn't make herself believe God still held the reins to her life. She couldn't stop the snort.

David faced her at the sound. "I don't have a problem with that, Gram. Don't know why, but for some reason He's seen fit to stick me with this assignment — with *her*. I'll do my job for Him, to bring Him honor, even if it kills me to deal with her."

Lauren bit her tongue to hold back something rude.

"It's a matter of trust," Grandma Dottie said, her voice no longer brisk and stern, but rather warm and caring.

Lauren wanted so much to reach out and take some of that love into her aching heart. But she couldn't. She couldn't trust anymore.

Grandma Dottie went on. "It boils down

to faith. Don't you believe Scripture? Don't you believe God will use everything to the good of those who love Him and whom He calls to his purpose?"

"You know I do, Gram."

Lauren felt a tug deep inside. Even as recently as this morning she would have had no problem with that question. But now, after that awful meeting with Audrey, after all she'd thought about on the drive here, after seeing David again —

She couldn't answer, so she didn't.

But Dottie refused to take silence for an answer. "Lauren? I understood you were a Christian. Are you? Do you trust God? Do you have any measure of faith?"

She looked down at the antique Persian rug at her feet. "I always have been a believer, and have always put my faith in the Lord. But now? After meeting *him?*" She pointed at David. "I don't know that I can find it in me to trust. Anyone. Anyone at all."

Grandma Dottie's sharp, indrawn breath ricocheted from wall to wall of the large room as though it had been cannon shot. "Have you lost your faith? Don't you trust God?"

Lauren searched her heart. What did she really think? Did she have any faith left?

Did she trust God? Was He even there for her to trust? If He was, then why was He letting all this happen to her? She'd never turned away from Him; she'd walked with Him for years.

If God was who she'd always believed Him to be, who the Bible said He was, then how could He have abandoned her when she needed Him most?

"I can't say what I know, what I doubt, who I trust. I don't know much of anything anymore. I only know who I can't trust."

She looked straight at David. "Look at it from my point of view. My big brother betrayed me. My colleague and former boss betrayed me. You? I don't think you ever cared one way or another, but I thought maybe I could trust you — if for no other reason than your job. Turns out I can't. I can't even trust that supposed stronghold of security and reliability, the all-powerful FBI. If God allowed all these betrayals, as it's obvious He did, then who is He? Where is He? How can I trust Him?"

"You need faith to see Him in the midst of trouble, Lauren," Grandma Dottie said. "You know it's all about trust. God didn't do any of these things to you. Flawed humans did. And He hasn't left you. Even if you may be leaving Him."

"But if God's in control, then He could have stopped it all. He didn't. He didn't keep the promises He made me in His Word."

She shuddered. She no longer felt the firm support of the ground beneath her feet. Everything that once had been familiar now felt tilted, skewed and distorted. "Even God's betrayed me. Why would you think I'd want to trust Him? How do you expect me to trust Him after all this?"

Her only response was the tear that rolled down Dottie Latham's lined cheek.

FIFTEEN

Walker leaned back in his chair. "Dinner was spectacular, Grandma Dottie."

"Isn't it always?" J.Z. patted his stomach.

David shot his grandmother a grin. "Hey, Gram. Ever think of opening a greasy spoon joint? You'd be a hit."

"Them's fightin' words, Davey-boy." She put on a fierce frown and threatened him with a serving spoon still decorated with small globs of mashed potatoes. "My food's never greasy. And since you don't cook, and you've got to keep body and soul together, you might not want to insult the cook that feeds you."

"Woo-hoo!" Walker crowed. "Give 'im what for, Grandma!"

"Diet time, Mr. I'm-a-Forever-Bachelor-Loner!" The newlywed J.Z. showed off his wife's beringed hand then waggled his ring finger with its own shiny gold band.

"No fair!" he cried. "Three — or more —

against one's not cool."

Mark scraped back his chair and flung himself at David's chest. "I'm with you, Monster Man."

Something warm, mushy and sweet filled his chest — yeah, like those sappy heart movies and poems he considered too bogus for words. But he couldn't deny the feeling. It was too strong and too real.

He ruffled the boy's hair. "All right, Mark Man. You and me, we're the good guys, and we're gonna whup their butts."

Mark giggled then covered his mouth with his hand. In a loud whisper, he said, "Watch it, Monster Man. That's a potty word. Aunt Lauren's gonna wash your mouth."

David glanced at the washerwoman, but found on her face the same stony expression she'd worn since the confrontation earlier that day. And while he shouldn't feel anything, a contrary part of him wanted to see her smile again, wanted to win her trust, wanted her to lean on him whenever troubles left her reeling and weak.

He'd known she was dangerous from the very start.

"Hey, Mark," he whispered. "How about you go give your aunt one of these awesome hugs? She looks like she really, really needs one."

That upset the boy. "Don't cry, Aunt Lauren. I'm still your friend."

Instead of the smile he'd hoped for, her eyes took on a wounded look, her cheeks lost their color, and her lips tightened to thin lines. David realized it wasn't her current problems that caused the pain, but rather the boy declaring himself David's ally.

Lauren saw David as the enemy.

Worse yet, she now saw the child's spontaneous show of affection as just one more betrayal. He'd come to know her well enough to read her. She felt she'd lost everything, even her nephew's love.

That ridiculously emotional new spot in his chest ached. He had to do something. He couldn't let Lauren continue to see herself alone, betrayed and cast away. He had to bring the beautiful warm smile back to her lips and the sparkle back to her crystal clear green eyes.

He had to figure out who was behind her recent troubles.

But he didn't know how — yet.

"I know you guys are dying to go hash out some spy stuff," Maryanne Prophet said. "And since I've had all the secret investigation mumbo jumbo I never did want in the first place, I'm going to the kitchen with Grandma."

234

Mark raised his head from its spot on Lauren's belly. "Cookies?"

Gram winked. "Come on up!"

Mark looked at his aunt, whose face revealed conflicting emotions. A small smile, probably a response to the mischief in Mark's eyes, softened the anguish and anger Lauren's features revealed. The pain in her eyes, well, he should probably take responsibility for that. And the reluctance in every fiber of her body most likely reflected the new conflict between Lauren and the Lord. Not to mention other Christians.

"Let's get cookies!" Mark told Lauren. He tugged on her hand, and even though her reluctance stayed put, she did follow him.

"Wow!" Walker shook his head as she left the room. "What a change."

J.Z. turned to David, arched a brow. "What's the deal? She hasn't said a word after her 'Hellos' when we got here."

"That's why I called you guys. I need to talk through this case, and I can't trust the office anymore."

J.Z. nodded. "I'm with you."

Walker frowned; wise men never took it lightly. "Am I hearing what I think I'm hearing?"

David met his gaze. "If you're hearing

mole, then you are."

"I've said it since the summer," J.Z. said. To Walker, he added, "Whoever it is almost cost Maryanne her life."

The intensity in J.Z.'s deep voice echoed what David had felt since Lauren told him about the visitor to the school. He wouldn't let anyone hurt her, no matter how far away she pushed him, no matter how determined those after her might be.

"Any idea who turned?" David asked.

J.Z. shook his head. "Wish I knew."

Walker barked out a rough laugh. "Man, am I glad I'm not that dude! When J.Z. gets that look. Watch out!"

David smiled, his predatory instincts also at the ready. "I'm glad he feels like I do. Whoever this is has already rammed a car at Lauren. And now he ruined her chances to get her job back."

"What do you mean?" J.Z. asked.

David told his friends about Lauren's afternoon. They agreed that something shady was coming down. He brought out a notebook, and for the next two hours the three men listed everything they knew about Lauren's situation.

When they still had nothing to show for their efforts, David's frustration got the better of him. He stood and paced.

"None of this makes sense. We must have missed something here. But what? Where's the missing link?"

Neither man answered.

Walker eventually leaned back and tipped the chair on two legs. "Where do we go from here?"

"You tell me. How far did you guys get with that truckload of paperwork you took from upstairs?"

"You don't remember? I told you we finished." He pointed at the notebook. "I put down everything we got from that mess. DiStefano dabbled in dirty laundry, mostly for Papparelli and a few of his 'family' members."

J.Z. tapped his pen against the table. "Seems pretty clear to me. We need to figure out what was so important in that missing file. Someone wanted it bad enough to take the whole thing from your office. And it looks like they didn't have much time. It would have been less risky and obvious if they made copies then left the file in place."

Walker laced his hands behind his head. "Either that or they don't care."

The gears in David's head picked up their pace. "If they don't care, then it means they're not afraid. They feel safe. The only way that's possible is if a higher-up is protecting them."

They fell silent again. David's thoughts ricocheted in his head. So much bounced around that he felt off-kilter, as if his feet had hit a slick patch of ice. He wondered if he'd ever find his balance again.

And now he understood Lauren's anger, her bitterness, her hopelessness. He, too, had been betrayed. Someone close to him, someone he worked with, maybe even had to trust his life to, had turned. But who? Why? And who did they work for?

He'd never known betrayal before. Now he felt its harsh bitter burn. What did he do next? How did he know who he could trust and who would sell him out?

He did know one thing. If he didn't have God's love and protection on his side, he might let discouragement and anger take over as Lauren had.

But what about her faith? Where did it go? How could she question the Father's love? Yeah, she'd hit a rotten time in her life, but this wasn't the time to dump the one and only reality, the single true thing in her life.

As he thought this through, he realized he knew one more thing. He wanted to help her recover her faith. It mattered to him. He wanted to help her get back to the comfort of the Lord's care.

"Hey!" Walker yelled.

David blinked. "What's the deal?"

"Not me, man. You're the one who wigged out on us. Where'd that brain of yours take off to?"

He shrugged. "Just thinking about this stuff."

"It's a mess, isn't it?" J.Z. commented.

"I'll say." Walker stood. "Why would DiStefano's dirtier friends or a mole among you feds want to hurt Lauren? Why would they risk their cover by stealing from your office? What's so important about that file?"

"And why would anyone, mole or otherwise, go to Lauren's last place of employment?" David asked. "She's a teacher. Not a likely target for the mob —"

"A mole," Lauren said from the open doorway. "You mean to tell me that someone in the FBI has something against me? Is out to get me?"

Was the mole working intentionally against Lauren? "I can't say," David answered. "I can tell you that someone stole my case file from my office. And someone, not me nor Walker or J.Z., went fishing for info at the school."

Her response made him wonder if she'd heard anything he'd said.

"And you wonder why I'm angry?" Her eyes flashed again, this time with rage. "Everyone's betrayed me. Even God. I don't believe He's out there watching over me. I don't even think He's anywhere anymore."

"Don't do that," David urged. "God's not the one who let you down. He's there, right where He's always been, and His heart's weeping for you. One or more of His children has turned his back on the Father's commandments. He's the one who's done you harm."

"Those are very pretty words, Agent Latham. But I'm not buying them anymore. And you might want to go back to preschool and learn to count all over again. It's more than just one jerk who's hit me when I'm down. I can only count on myself. Well, Mark and me. We'll make it on our own. We have to."

"Lonely way to live," J.Z. said in a soft voice. "I should know. I shut God out of my life because of my earthly father's crimes for years."

Interest softened the harshness in her stare. "Your father's a criminal?"

"He's doing life for murder one. And he earned it the old-fashioned way. He killed for a living."

She took a sharp breath. "The mob."

"You got it." J.Z. walked to her side and placed a gentle hand on her shoulder. "I blamed God for my father's criminal behavior, for the sins he committed, for the trial that followed, and my mother's death during that trial. I thought I had to go it alone to prevent any more betrayals."

"J.Z., honey . . ." Maryanne hurried to her husband's side, a world of love in her eyes. "Are you sure you want to talk about —"

"Yeah, I am." He wrapped his free arm around his wife's waist. "Maybe God's been waiting for me to reach just this point."

"That seems more cruel than loving and wise," Lauren said, her voice again tough as steel. "God would let your life and family be devastated just so you could . . . what? Tell me I should trust Him when He's let my life get crushed? What kind of God would do that? Why? Why should I trust Him?"

"I think He may have brought us all here tonight to redeem what happened to my family. Maybe you need to know I'm the one who left God, not the other way around."

David watched Lauren struggle with that thought. "The Father sees more than any of us can," he said. "He's brought you a couple

241

of new friends to encourage you along this rough patch you've hit."

"You mean the rough patch He let you and others build in front of me."

"Hey, man. Leave the lady alone." Walker's deep bass voice echoed in the silent room. "She's not ready to listen. She's hardened her spirit, and we can all spout bits and pieces of our testimony, but she'll only close her heart more with everything we say."

David glared. "So what do you want us to do? Just sit back and let her hurt? What about the compassion we're supposed to show our brothers and sisters in Christ?"

Walker shrugged. "All we can do is offer. She said 'No, thank you.' The Father never did tell us to shove it down anyone's throat."

"But He did say we should bind one another's wounds. Lauren's hurting —"

"Thanks to you," she bit off then turned and ran from the room.

He went to follow her, but Walker held him back. "Let her go, brother. She's just not ready to listen right now. You say she's a Christian?"

"She told me she has been all her life. Didn't she talk about her faith when you were here? That's why I can't believe this change. It worries me."

"She'll come back when she realizes life's

not worth living outside the Almighty's love," Grandma Dottie said. "Sometimes, we have to hurt, and hurt a lot, before we're ready to see that God's been right there with us, waiting for us, all along."

He forced himself to open his clenched fists. He looked at his friends then toward the hallway where Lauren had disappeared. "I'm not giving up on her. I won't let anyone get to her again. I'm going to find out what the deal is with the late and not-so-great Ric DiStefano. And I'm going to prove to her she can trust me no matter what."

J.Z. chuckled. "Boy, are you in trouble."

Maryanne leaned against her husband's shoulder. "Mmm-hmm."

"She's pretty cool," Walker offered, a grin on his face. "When she's not mad at God. You know."

Grandma Dottie tsk-tsked. "I think it's time for you boys to be on your way. We need some peace and quiet here. Lauren has to hear God's voice, and she won't be able to do that with all your shoptalk, your stories and your goofy jokes."

"You're so right, Grandma," Maryanne said. "Lauren needs time alone to let her anger chill a bit. Come on, J.Z. Chauffeur me home already."

They exchanged good nights, everyone agreed to pray for Lauren, and together headed for the front door. Gram went upstairs after she hugged and prayed travel mercies for all.

Then J.Z. got that familiar gleam back in his gaze. David knew to duck when it showed up, since it meant trouble of one kind or another. But this time he had nowhere to go. He didn't even know what was coming, so he couldn't concoct a change of subject to get the heat off his back. Then, too, they were guests at his family home. Hospitality and all that.

"Tell you what, David," his fellow Special Agent said. "We'll pray for you, too."

Relief made him smile. "Thanks. This has turned out to be a tougher case than I expected."

J.Z. grinned. "Oh, you'll do fine on the case. I just think you'd better take some time and go shopping."

"Are you nuts? I'm not the shopping therapy kind."

"You don't need therapy, brother," Walker said with a chuckle. "What you need is a set of wedding bands."

Then they left. David stayed, mouth agape.

He would never dignify that comment

with a response.

They really were out of their minds. Crazy. Loco. Round the bend nuts.

Weren't they?

Lauren rushed Mark through his bedtime routine. Lately it seemed she'd gotten in the habit of cutting short the warm pattern she'd established for him. But she had so much on her mind, and her emotions were in such turmoil, that she was afraid she might influence the child. This wasn't the right kind of influence to have on him.

Once he dozed off, she went to the room Grandma Dottie had insisted was hers for as long as she wanted. Even after all the rough moments of the day and the pain of betrayal, the elegant bedroom felt like a sanctuary.

The silky cream jacquard comforter beckoned, as did the pile of cushy pillows propped against the padded and button-tufted headboard. She didn't fight the pull. In seconds, she'd changed out of her clothes and into her favorite flannel nightgown, and slipped into the luxurious cocoon.

At first, sleep refused to come. But after long moments of determined relaxation, coupled with a ruthless eviction of trouble-some thoughts, Lauren finally fell asleep.

Hours later, an anguished cry woke her up. Her heart pounded in her chest, and fear knotted her throat.

What was that? Was someone hurt? Had Grandma Dottie fallen down the long, curved staircase?

She left the bed and stepped into her squishy, fleece-lined slippers. As she walked out to the hall, she heard the cry again.

"Mark!"

Lauren hurried to her nephew's bedroom, her heart in her throat. She scolded herself for her selfish behavior earlier that evening. Had she missed something? Had she denied him the comfort he needed to sleep through the night? Was he sick?

When she ran into the room, she saw Mark tangled in a noose of sheets and blankets, his eyes open wide with fear.

"Another bad dream?" she asked and drew him into her arms.

He nodded his head against her shoulder.

"Don't let it scare you, honey. I'm here, and you're okay."

He sobbed, his little hands fisted in the soft rose-colored flannel of her nightgown. She again realized how young he was, even though he tried so hard to be a "grown-big boy" during the day.

"Come on, sweetheart. Lie down. You

need to rest. Aunt Lauren's not going anywhere until you're sleeping like a log again."

"No! Don't go. Stay with me."

"But we don't fit in this bed, Mark. And you need the space so you can fall asleep again."

"No! Pleeeze."

"Okay, okay. We'll see what we can work out." Lauren drew in a deep breath. "Why are you so scared, honey? There's nothing here that's going to hurt you."

"I like Grandma Dottie's house."

"Then forget the dream. Don't let it bug you."

He hiccupped. "It was really bad."

"Tell me about it?"

"Uncle Don and Daddy were yelling."

That caught her by surprise. "Are you sure it was Uncle Don in your dream?"

"I'm sure."

"Why were they yelling? Do you remember?"

He began to shake his head, slowly at first then harder and faster. "No! I don't know anything. I dinn'nt see it. I *dinn'nt* see it!"

Mark's voice grew shriller with growing fear. Lauren set her curiosity aside. "All right, kiddo. I get it. Just relax and go back to sleep. I won't leave you."

She laid him back in the bed, pulled up the covers and tucked him in. She perched on the edge of the mattress, and rubbed the little boy's back. But no matter how long she stroked him, no matter how quietly she sat, he never did close his green eyes.

"Aunt Lauren?" he finally said.

"Yes."

"C'n we pray?"

She gasped. What could she say? Should she pass her anger and doubts to him? Would it be the right thing to do? Did she believe he'd be better off as a faithless child?

"Yeah, Aunt Lauren," David said from the doorway. "That sounds like a great idea to me. Let's all hold hands and pray."

She met his gaze, and the gentle concern there hit her right in the heart. She couldn't turn him down. Not in front of Mark.

Liar! a corner of her much-too-honest conscience yelled.

She couldn't turn David down, but not because of Mark. She couldn't turn him down because of what she felt when he looked at her that way.

As angry as she was, as little as she trusted him, when he looked at her with that much kindness and warmth, she no longer felt alone. Her rage eased. Her bitterness mellowed.

In the morning she'd have to steel herself against his appeal all over again, but now, in the dark, after Mark's troubled sleep had made any more sleep impossible for her, she couldn't reject David's offer for prayer.

Even if she couldn't pray.

For Mark's sake, she took David's and then the boy's hand, bowed her head and listened to the earnest praise and fervent pleas David offered the King she'd once served.

Sixteen

The next morning Lauren woke up with a start. Her first surprise came when she realized she had slept after all. Mark's nightmare and David's prayers had left her nerves frayed, and she'd thought she'd never fall asleep again. But by the grace of —

She caught herself. She didn't want to go there.

What mattered was that she had slept.

The second surprise came from the loud metal banging and clanging just below her room. Since it was the foyer, she wondered if Grandma Dottie had received some kind of interesting delivery, maybe oversize Christmas gifts or a new appliance.

Either way, the morning wouldn't wait for her. She had to get up. As she stepped into her slippers, Mark burst into the room.

"Aunt Lauren! You gotta see Grandma Dottie and Cousin Bea."

Cousin Bea? She smiled. Those ladies were

something else. "What are they up —"

He answered with a slammed bedroom door on his way out.

More interesting sounds came from below, and Lauren showered and dressed quickly. What could they be up to?

At the foot of the spectacular staircase, she came to a screeching halt. Ladders, buckets, drop cloths, rollers, paintbrushes, scrapers, rags, and a smattering of additional odd items Lauren couldn't identify spread across the gorgeous parquet floor.

The two tall ladders wore sassy, unpredictable old ladies on their top rungs.

" 'Morning, Lauren!"

"How'd you sleep, honey?"

"I slept okay, but probably not as well as you two. What are you doing?"

Grandma Dottie tapped the ceiling. "See the lumpy, bumpy stuff up here?"

Lauren looked at the fluffy white frosting-like surface. "Sure, I see it. What are you doing to it?"

"My husband was a stubborn old mule." Grandma Dottie shook her head, but the tender smile on her lips softened the criticism. "When we had to have the wiring updated, the electricians chopped up a whole lot of the ceiling in the process. He wanted the 'modern' finish instead of the restored plaster I wanted."

"So they wound up with cruddy popcorn ceilings." Bea scraped a metal spatula across the offensive surface. "*Everyone* knows that Christopher Lowell, Hildi, Frank, Candace Olsen, Doug and Kenneth Brown scrape off this stuff first when they're redoing a room."

"Who are those people?" Lauren asked.

Both women stared at her as if she'd just sprouted a dozen heads. "What?" she asked. "What's wrong? What did I say?"

"You don't know *the* designers?"

"I've never dealt with a designer."

"Pshaw!" Grandma Dottie rolled her eyes. "Who needs them? I've never worked with one of them, either. It's more fun to do it yourself. But I am an HGTV junky, and I watch all the design shows I can get on my satellite dish."

"Hey!" Bea cried. "Don't forget who got you hooked on 'em in the first place."

Grandma Dottie gave a slight bow. "Oh, Madam TV Poobah! I'm forever indebted. How could I have lived on if you hadn't shared your addiction? Ignorance *isn't* bliss."

Lauren laughed. "Is there anything I can do to help?"

"Do you know what we're doing?"

"Haven't got a clue, but I do learn pretty quickly."

252

Grandma Dottie looked at her one heart-beat longer than Lauren thought necessary. What would the outspoken senior come up with next?

"I sure hope you do learn fast." Then she pointed to a pile of items a few feet away from her perch. "You can start by filling the squirt bottles."

Lauren spent the next hour running errands for the elderly decorators. She refilled bottles, found glop bowls, rinsed washcloths when they gunked up too much, and generally put herself at the ladies' beck and call.

Even Mark stayed busy. He shuttled between Saturday-morning cartoons and the spectacle in the foyer, Ochiban at his heels. But eventually, Lauren had enough of the gofer job.

"How about if I take a turn at the popcorn?" she asked. "I've watched you both, and it doesn't take a rocket scientist to do it. Besides, I'm just a little bored watching the two of you have all the fun!"

Bea crowed. "Toldja we'd win her over to our side. See? It didn't take a whole lot of time, and now she wants to take over our jobs."

"I never doubted you," Grandma Dottie answered. "I just thought we'd have to sweet-talk her a whole lot more. But this is way cool beans. We can always use help."

"Okay, ladies. *She* has a question for you. Do you have an extra ladder?"

"Nope." Bea scampered down. "But I beat Dottie to the ground, so here." She thrust her scraper toward Lauren. "Sub for me first."

Grandma Dottie raised her hands in defeat. "All right, all right. But you have to help me move the ladder over to this corner. I finished all I can reach right in front of the door."

"You sure you want to go back there?" Lauren asked. "What if someone swings the door into you."

"Nah. It's locked, I don't expect anyone today, and you guys know I'm where I am. Just be careful if for some reason you do have to open it."

Lauren handed Bea the empty squirt bottle. While she waited, she scraped popcorn goop off the metal spatula and into the half-filled plastic bowl. As soon as her gofer returned, she grabbed the squirter and went to work on the lumpy texture.

The actual job proved even easier than she'd thought, and she'd never thought it difficult. It was, though, time-consuming and mind-numbingly boring. She could see where, if one had to do the work alone, it might never get done.

But with the Bea-and-Dottie comedy team in house, the time went by faster than she realized.

"I'm hungry," Mark said after a while. "When're we having lunch?"

Bea ruffled his hair. "We got you covered, Mark Man. Follow me to the kitchen."

No sooner had they left, than the doorbell rang. "I'll get it," Lauren offered, afraid Grandma Dottie might try to hurry down the ladder.

She opened the door to an angry Don D'Amato. "Hi, Don —"

"Don't give me that." His cheeks grew redder and his eyes narrowed further. "I'm not here on a social call."

A niggle of fear hit Lauren. In all the years she'd known him, she'd never seen Don like this. She was alone with two senior citizens and a five-year-old child. Then she remembered Mark's bad dream. Don and Ric had been arguing, and it had been intense enough to traumatize the boy into ongoing nightmares. Could the dream come from a real event he witnessed?

The frightening possibility would have to be considered at another time. Her hands shook, but she didn't want to show fear.

She managed a calm voice. "How can I help you?"

"You can call off your . . . your . . ." He floundered for a moment longer, then continued. "I don't know what the guy might really be. But I do know he's no mover."

David! She played for time. "I don't know what you mean."

Don stepped into the doorway, looming closer, in an obvious effort to intimidate her. "Ric always said you were brilliant," he said. "Don't make a liar of your brother. Of course you know who that fake mover-from-on-high is. You had him stashed in your attic, and now he's turned up everywhere I've gone for the last few days. Wonder if he's the one who took it upon himself to ransack my office last night?"

She would have had to use a steak knife to cut through the thick sarcasm in his voice. "I have no idea who went through your office, Don." She didn't; David would have been more discreet than to ransack. "But you can be sure it wasn't me. I'm too busy looking for a job and taking care of Mark. Oh, and don't forget I've had to move, too."

"I'm not buying any sob story from you. I bet your 'mover' moved you here, into his pricey place. You should be ashamed of yourself. Think of the effect your actions will have on Mark."

The choked croak from behind the door reminded Lauren she wasn't alone. Don didn't seem to hear it.

He went on. "Who cares what you do? I just want you to tell your snoopy playmate to stay out of my life. If I have any more nighttime 'visitors' or if I see him around my house again, I know now where I can come get him."

"But there's no man here —"

"Zip it, Lauren. Your big green eyes don't look so innocent anymore. Just tell the guy to leave me alone. I have nothing he might want."

He made a grand gesture with his arms. "Just look around." He pointed to various details. "He's got a fortune. I don't. Besides, we still live in America, don't we? Our country protects a man's right to privacy. I've got mine, and your sugar daddy's got his here —" another wide, encompassing gesture "— with all his money, his trophy and his treasures —"

"Aaack!" Grandma Dottie toppled over when Don's arm smacked the door. Lauren went to help her.

Don cursed. "This is disgusting."

Lauren checked her hostess's arms and legs for broken bones. "If you're done insulting me, then please go. Your loss of control made you knock an elderly woman off a ladder, and if she's injured, you could be in for assault-and-battery charges. Not to mention defamation of my character. I'm sure you of all people know about all that."

"What do you mean me? I bet she did this on purpose, too. And *you* dare to threaten *me?*"

"You're delusional. We were here, minding our business. You stormed in like a mad bull into a fighting ring and knocked her off the ladder."

Satisfied nothing critical had happened to Grandma Dottie, Lauren finally looked up at Don. And she couldn't stop the laughter. Splotches of gray-white popcorn slime made him look like an angry giant molting rabbit.

"It's not funny!" the rabbit roared then rubbed more dreck from his face. "You're insane on top of everything else."

Footsteps ran down the hallway. "Uncle Don! You look gross!"

He scraped the last soggy blob of popcorn crud off one eyebrow, gave the boy a dirty look, glared again at Lauren and turned to leave. "Who in her right mind hangs out at the top of a ladder behind a door?"

"Someone who's working on her ceiling, buddy boy," that someone countered. "And you and your dirty mouth and mind are not welcome here. If you don't vamoose right now, I'm calling the cops. Maybe the state troopers, too. I'd go so far as to get the FBI, CIA, National Guard and Special Forces if they'll get rid of you."

"I'm outta here, but she'd better get the message to her 'mover.' I see him again, or see that someone's been where they shouldn't be, and she'll regret it."

"Is that a threat?" Lauren asked, her own temper rising now.

"Read it however you want." He slammed the door as he left.

Lauren plopped on the floor next to David's grandmother. Mark moaned, then ran into Lauren's arms, his sobs heartrending. Grandma Dottie sat up.

"Where's your cell phone?" she asked. "Mine's charging up in my room."

Lauren dug it out of her pocket and tossed it over. "I hope you're calling David."

Grandma Dottie snorted. "Who'd you think I'd be calling? Santa Claus?"

"Hah!" Bea said, a zip-top plastic bag full of ice in hand. "You're kinda late, girls. Davey's on his way. I gave him a ringy-dingy back in the kitchen. I figured I'd be more help if that idiot didn't know I was around."

Lauren gave Bea a thankful smile. "You both are great."

Bea and Lauren helped Grandma Dottie to the living room and onto the comfortable settee, placed the ice on a sore hip, and then returned to the foyer. In silence, they cleaned up the spilled schmutz from the ceiling. Finally, David arrived.

The three women brought him up to speed, each one from her own perspective. In a short time, he left for the office to make a report. And yes, he had followed Don to get some idea of his activities, but he hadn't broken into the office. Another mystery.

Had that person also gone to Lauren's school? And who was he?

Answers didn't come. The days before Christmas passed by as Lauren waited and read the want ads. She went to a mall for gifts, picked up something for the daunting duo, and yes, even a present for David. Mark was easy to shop for. He loved anything mechanical, especially robots, as his love for Ochiban showed.

And then it was Christmas Eve. Lauren could find no reasonable way to avoid attending church services with Grandma Dottie, Bea and David. They anticipated the celebration of their Lord's birth with faith and joy. Mark's excitement over Jesus's birthday made her feel like Scrooge, since her bitterness hadn't lessened, but rather grew each day her situation remained the same.

In church, she wound up sitting next to David. The chances of it being coincidental were nil. Grandma Dottie and Bea looked too smug for her to consider anything but rampant matchmaking as the order of the day.

Then the organ filled the sanctuary with its rich, lush tones. Lauren tried to steel herself against participating, but the familiar Christmas carols and hymns tugged at her, made her yearn, and before long, she lifted her voice with the rest of the congregation. David held the hymnbook for both of them to use.

She struggled with the sermon. The pastor spoke of God's gifts, his generous blessings and his encompassing love. With all Lauren had gone through in the last few weeks, she felt even worse when she heard the promises she'd always treasured but no longer could trust.

Every second that went by, she became more aware of David's solid warmth at her side. On the one hand, his presence did make her feel safer in some ways. But something about him affected her in ways she didn't want. There was no denying his love for his grandmother, his deep faith and his single-minded focus on his job. Any woman would find these traits as appealing as his clean-cut good looks.

On the other hand, she wasn't convinced he hadn't been the one who'd spoken with Audrey. He had followed Don, and could conceivably have rifled the law office. Would he have left obvious signs of his search? He might have if he'd been in a hurry or if someone had shown up unexpectedly.

What troubled her most about David was the emotions he brought to life in her whenever he interacted with Mark. At those times, she could only see the gentle side of him, that side a woman might trust. Those feelings led to danger.

She couldn't afford to fall for David Latham.

She couldn't trust anyone again.

The service finished with Handel's "Hallelujah Chorus." The Latham party regrouped back at the beautifully decorated — and popcorn-ceiling-free — family home, where they were in for an experience. Dessert at Grandma Dottie's was an event.

"Would you be a dear and please bring

me the vanilla ice cream?" Grandma asked Lauren the minute they closed the front door.

"Sure, and I'll be quick." Then, when she reached the freezer in the basement, she heard heavy footsteps come down the stairs. A moment later, David bent to avoid the low floor joists.

"Is there a problem?" she asked.

"Maybe, if you can't ignore Gram and Bea's ham-handed efforts." With a wry grin, he shook his head. "Gram said she forgot to tell you she wanted the ice-cream cake, too, and asked me to bring it up."

Lauren winced. "That's a whole lot of ice cream."

"And a whole lot of Gram's meddling."

She opened the freezer and took out the large bucket of vanilla. "Does she do this a lot?"

He pulled out the boxed cake. "It's her favorite pastime. She's determined to marry me off. I'm surprised she hasn't bugged you before this."

Lauren chuckled. "Who has she foisted on you up to now?"

David rolled his eyes, and Lauren noticed for the first time how much he resembled his grandmother but in a very masculine way. "Would you believe she hangs out with a bunch of crazy women who spend a couple of evenings a month at Lady Look Lovely cosmetics parties?"

"No way!"

"Yeah, way. I don't know if she actually buys the stuff, but that's her favorite evening gig."

"Please tell me she doesn't have one of her elderly buddies in mind for you."

He gave her a mock glare. "Don't you dare give her any ideas! She hasn't up to now, but who knows what she might come up with, even if it's just from a stray thought of yours?"

"I'd have to put it in words first."

"Yeah, and thinking something is only a nanosecond from saying it."

With the ice cream in one hand, she started toward the stairs. She paused, used her free hand to zip up her mouth, and then chuckled. "You know. You've just given me a fantastic weapon. I can hold it over your head — it might even keep you on the up-and-up."

He grew serious. "I've always been on the up-and-up, Lauren. From that night in the street, I've done nothing but try to keep you and Mark safe. Yes, my boss assigned me to the DiStefano case as a whole, and in the beginning I didn't know much about you.

You could've killed your brother for all I knew back then."

Her anger knew no bounds. "How could you say something like that —"

"Easy, there. I only stated a possibility. We knew nothing about you. Your brother, a shady character, was dead, but you told me he'd been behind the wheel of the car that hit you. Tell me you wouldn't find that suspicious if you'd been in my shoes."

When he put things in those terms, Lauren couldn't deny the truth. "I'd really like to tell you I would never have suspected anything, but I like to stay on the side of truth. You're right. I probably would have found the whole thing pretty fishy."

"Thanks. You don't know how much that means to me."

"What?"

"That you're at least willing to listen to what I have to say. And that you're even willing to give me the benefit of the doubt."

"I don't wear blinders, David."

"Good to hear."

They went up the stairs in silence, and the rest of the evening unfolded in a spirit of holiday cheer. Lauren found it impossible to cling to her anger and bitterness when so much love and joy surrounded her.

Mark's bedtime came, and she tucked him

in. To her surprise, David joined them just as she patted the blanket around his small body.

"Can I join your prayers?" he asked.

Mark picked his head up off the pillow. "You bet, Monster Man. Here."

David held the boy's hand then extended his other one to Lauren. She hesitated, sat next to Mark on the side of the bed, and when she couldn't put it off any longer, she took David's hand.

His fingers were strong and warm, and his gentle touch felt almost like a balm. Then he began to pray. His rich baritone rose and fell with words of praise and devotion. He asked blessings on everyone gathered in the home, and he prayed for peaceful, happy dreams for Mark.

At his Amen, Mark whispered, "I love you, Monster Man."

A knot formed in Lauren's throat. What a precious moment! For a long time she'd longed for a family of her own, but she'd reached a point where she accepted her single state. She'd welcomed the chance to mother Mark, and felt that a husband would show up if the Lord —

She shook her head. That wasn't where she wanted to go.

A glance at David showed unexpected

dampness in his eyes. He cleared his throat then said, "I love you, too, Mark. I really do."

Tears spilled from Lauren's eyes. At that moment she recognized her need to hear those words again, this time, meant for her. Only for her. But it wasn't to be. At least not from anyone but Mark.

She couldn't trust anyone that much again.

A soft touch on her cheek drew her gaze back to David. He'd wiped off one of her tears. The hand still wrapped around hers tightened a touch, just enough to tell her he shared the emotion of the moment.

At least he couldn't know her thoughts.

When she looked down at Mark, she realized he'd already dozed off. "I hope he sleeps the whole night through," she whispered as she and David left the room.

"Has he had more nightmares?"

"Every night."

"What are they about?"

"He will only say that Ric and Don had an argument, and that he doesn't know anything."

"Hmm . . ."

She took note of his thoughtful expression. "Care to share the meaning of that 'Hmm . . .'?"

"Not until I check out something I just thought of."

She didn't like that answer, but she knew better than to argue. "Fair enough. But remember you once agreed to tell me what you learned that affected us."

"You're right. I did. And as soon as I check this out, I'll get back to you."

They reached the dining room, where the goodies already had been put away. All that remained of their dessert banquet was the large urn Grandma Dottie had filled with sweet, spiced apple cider. The cold night was perfect for another cup.

Lauren poured one for herself then glanced at David. "Do you want some?"

"Oh, yeah. It'll hit the spot tonight."

They carried their hot mugs into the living room, expecting to find the daunting duo there, but found the room empty. The fire in the hearth had burned down low, and it had obviously warmed the pine garland that dressed the mantel in holiday cheer. The scent of the sap wafted through the room.

Christmas tree lights flickered tiny and white. The presents underneath, with their colorful gift wrap and shiny bows, spoke of plenty and generosity. The comfortable, elegant furniture invited Lauren to curl up for a while, watch the low flames, and just soak in the peace. She wondered if the anger and bitterness would let her.

David took a seat in a large wing chair near the settee Lauren chose. As they sipped, they talked, but not about murder, accidents, break-ins, jobs or birds. They traded details of favorite childhood holiday celebrations; they compared favorite dishes; they laughed over each other's funniest memories; and they described favorite Christmas gifts.

She hadn't expected to feel anything besides fear and anger, but to her amazement, peace did fill her. After long, silent moments, she turned to David.

"Thanks."

"You're welcome. For what?"

She stared at her hands. "For one of the nicest Christmas Eves I can remember."

"It has been nice, hasn't it?"

"You've given me the gift of calm in the middle of the storm my life's become. I can't tell you how much that means to me."

"Does that mean you no longer see me as your enemy?"

She bit her lower lip. "I don't know, David. I really don't know anything these days."

"I'm sorry you feel that way, but I can

almost understand."

She chuckled. "Try a little harder, then. I'm sure you'll get there."

"What if I don't want to? What if I want to prove to you I'm really on your side? That all I want is to take care of you and Mark, and see you smile again?"

She felt her cheeks go warm. "That's very nice, but . . ."

"But you can't trust."

"Something like that."

"I don't give up easily," he said, his voice deep and serious. "And I always pray. You've been in my prayers since that night on the street, and you're not likely to leave anytime soon. God's still in the miracle business."

She drew a deep breath. "I don't know what to say —"

"Then don't say anything."

"But —"

His finger on her lips cut off her words. "Don't ruin it. It's been a beautiful evening, and I want to keep it that way. I'll tell you good night, go back out to my place, and see you in the morning. Okay?"

"Sure. Good night."

Then he leaned down, tipped her face up and lightly pressed his lips to hers. Before she could react, the kiss had ended.

But its effect lingered. She could feel the

gentle caress as they walked to the front door, as she locked up behind him, as she went upstairs, and as she fell asleep.

It even filled her dreams.

On Christmas morning, Lauren's alarm clock went off at six o'clock, just as she'd set it to do. She changed in a hurry, put on her coat, boots and gloves, then hurried to the garage out back of the stately old home. She'd stored the bicycle she'd bought Mark behind Grandma Dottie's Hummer, and wanted to bring it indoors before Mark had a chance to wake up.

But when she opened the heavy wooden door, she froze. The horror she found in the garage surpassed anything she could ever have imagined.

She screamed. Again and again terror pushed the screams out from deep inside. Her voice rose higher and shriller.

She closed her eyes.

She tried deep slow breaths.

She looked again, but nothing had changed.

"Lauren, dear!" Grandma Dottie said as she hurried to Lauren's side. "What's wrong?"

The shaking started in her hands. Then her legs felt boneless and weak. Finally, as she turned, the tears flooded her face, her head swam, and she knew she was on her way down.

"That man." She'd never forget how he looked. "His body . . ."

Lifeless, broken and tortured; Aloysius would never come looking for his bird again. Someone had made sure of that.

As everything went black, Lauren's last thought was of David.

What had he done? In trying to protect her and Mark, had he followed Aloysius as he'd followed Don? Had he caught the strange man skulking around the back of the house?

Was he responsible for this Christmas-morning murder?

SEVENTEEN

It would take years for Lauren to put the nightmares in the past. Her sympathy for Mark and his troubled sleep grew even greater.

No matter how she worked to banish it, the image of the dead Aloysius remained etched in her mind. She felt so numb that she barely noted the rush of activity after she'd made her gruesome discovery. David arrived minutes after Grandma Dottie came to her aid, and with the older woman's and his help, Lauren had gone back to the house. The police showed up minutes later.

She shook worse than any leaf in a tornado's winds the whole time they investigated the scene of the crime.

Still disoriented, she responded to the police officers' questions in a daze. David and J.Z. had a list of different ones that she also answered. But aside from the day Aloysius had come to her — Ric's — house, she'd never seen the man. And she knew nothing about the bird business.

J.Z. even questioned Mark. The boy, of course, didn't know a thing about the man or his fowl, as Grandma Dottie put it. If Lauren hadn't thought David's grandmother a terrific lady, she would've become a believer now. The older woman handled Mark's fears with the kind of ferocious protectiveness and generous love Lauren imagined she would lavish on a great-grandson of her own.

Lauren was almost — almost — sure Grandma Dottie hadn't had anything to do with David's questionable actions.

And even though she couldn't make herself trust him, she now hesitated to think he could have gone out of his way to do her harm. Christmas Eve had become a bright, shining memory, a moment to treasure.

But she couldn't live in a memory or in the long-gone past. Lauren wanted to move forward with her life; she was ready. So two days after Christmas, she grabbed one of Mark's Christmas presents she had to exchange, and got ready to head to the mall.

"Where do you think you're going?" Grandma Dottie winked. "Without me."

Lauren grinned. "To the moon and back. Actually, I'm going to exchange the jacket that didn't fit Mark."

"Not by yourself you're not."

Lauren knew better than to argue when Grandma Dottie's mind was made up. "So what army are you sending out with me?"

She blinked. Lauren thought something had clicked in the older woman's mind. Hmm . . . What could she be up to?

But all David's grandmother said was, "Me. I don't want you out there alone. The buddy system gives you lots of protection."

"I don't doubt your powers of intervention. But if we're both going out, what do you suggest we do with Mark? You know he won't want to come with us."

"Did you forget Bea? She's nuts about your little rascal, and he thinks she's another preschool playmate."

Lauren laughed. "Oh, I've noticed that and more. The three of you are something. You and Bea have been wonderful to him. I don't know what I would have done without all your help and generosity —"

" 'Inasmuch as ye have done it unto one of the least of these my brethren, ye have done it unto me.' "

Something churned in Lauren's stomach. "So you were just carrying out a Biblical command."

"Yes, honey. 'The greatest of these is love.'

275

Don't forget, before you or I were born, God loved us and sacrificed His Son for us. The least we can do is sacrifice a little of our time and energy and love one another in His name."

That internal tug-of-war started up again inside Lauren. The familiar teachings of the faith rang with authority. The reality of the last month, however, fought a pitched battle against that faith. Did God love her enough to protect her? If He did, where had He been? Where was He on Christmas morning?

She had nothing to say, so she shrugged.

Grandma Dottie sighed. "You're a tough nut to crack. Just like my stubborn David. The two of you are perfect for each other."

Before Lauren could object, the senior troublemaker charged out of the room. "See ya in the Hummer."

A half hour later, the Hummer straddled two parking spots at the mall — the enormous vehicle didn't fit in just one. Grandma Dottie hopped down from the stratospherically high running board and locked up with a click of her remote.

"All right! Shopping therapy's where it's at, girl. Let's go check out some cool stuff."

They walked into the crowded mall, and Lauren worked hard to keep up with David's grandmother. First, they hit the frozen yogurt stand for Grandma Dottie's swirl cone. Then they swerved into the kitchen paraphernalia store. There, Grandma Dottie found a gadget that, if one believed the hype on the box, did everything including cook and serve the meal.

"Gotta have it," she said. "One of those hoity-toity chefs on the Food Network used it to make a whole dinner. I'm kinda skeptical about it all, but it looked like so much fun. Can't wait to get it in my kitchen and see if it does what they say."

She filled a shopping cart with 'for my Lady Look Lovely girls' kitchen loot before she headed to the cashier. They examined every window display on their way to the children's store where Lauren bought the jacket. But partway there, Grandma Dottie just had to pop into the pet store.

"I never come to the mall without visiting those poor little critters. I usually buy one to take to my local vet. He has an adoption service, and we work together on some matchmaking."

Lauren wasn't going to touch that word with a cue stick — the last window display that had caught the exuberant senior's attention before they reached the pet store.

"Tell you what," she said. "Why don't I

go to the kids' store while you choose your next project? Then we can go grab soft drinks and head back to Bea and Mark."

"Sounds like a plan. I have to take my time to find the right critter. You know, the neediest one."

"Go for it." Wow! Was she sounding a lot like her slang-loving companion or what? "And I'll make sure the kiddo's winter jacket fits."

As she hurried to the store, the traditional "Carol of the Bells" played over the mall's PA system. Before she realized it, she'd begun to sing along, a smile on her face.

It took only minutes to make the jacket swap; the store was less crowded than she'd expected. With the bright primary-colored bag in hand, she went back out into the common area.

The next thing she knew, something sharp bit into her back through the fabric of her wool coat. "Don't try nothing funny," a harsh, male voice whispered in her ear. "You're coming with me. Take me to the kid."

Lauren's eyes widened. *He wanted Mark! How was she going to get out of this?*

"He's not with me."

The man jabbed his weapon deeper into her, but didn't speak.

She tried again. "Who are you?"

He pushed her forward. "Never mind me. Don't think you're gonna get away from me, 'cause you won't. I got you good, and we're going for the kid. Otherwise . . ."

She didn't need any more elaboration. But she had no intention to do what he wanted. She was ready to die if it would keep Mark safe. But she didn't want to just give in and give up.

Because of the holiday crowds and the concern over the possibility of terrorism at crowded so-called soft targets, the large mall had an obvious security presence. If she could create a commotion in front of one of those armed guards, she had a chance to make a run for it.

As it turned out, she didn't have to do much of anything other than react. A bevy of women rushed toward the guard at the corner of the jewelry store five feet away. One of them collapsed at the guy's feet and startled Lauren's captor.

He stumbled.

She spun away from his grasp.

"Hey!" he hollered. "Get back here."

Lauren did just that, but, so as not to be outdone by Grandma Dottie and friends, she swung her handbag and clobbered the stout man in the face. He howled and dropped the knife he'd used on Lauren to clutch his bloody nose.

"Ow!" He hopped from foot to foot while innocent bystanders stared in awe. He was a sight to behold. A three-hundred-or-so-pound man dancing, screaming and swabbing his face with a white handkerchief in the middle of a Christmas-decorated mall . . . it was the stuff of comedy movies.

Then Grandma Dottie took charge of the situation. "C'mon, girls!"

The "girls" went into action. One took the plastic lid off her extra large drink and sloshed it under the howler's feet. He caught an ice cube under the heel of a descending shoe and skidded sideways. A beehive-haired dynamo hurtled forward.

"Eee-yah!" she yelled as she crashed into him. "Go ahead, skazoid. Make my day!"

Grandma Dottie's pal bounced off the well-upholstered would-be kidnapper. He in turn bounced off the balcony railing then righted himself. When Lauren realized he was about to run, she dropped her shopping bag and purse, and followed the senior citizen's example.

She lunged for her attacker, but instead of ramming him in the side, she held out her arms, elbows braced, and hit him from behind.

He "Ooofed," and from the corner of her eye, she watched a lime-green-clad leg jut in front of the guy's feet as he tried to take another step. He stumbled, tripped over the colorful obstacle and went down on his face.

"Not again," he wailed.

For good measure, Lauren grabbed a pudgy wrist and yanked it up his back as she'd seen in movies and TV. He bellowed some more.

David ran up, followed by a platoon of security officers. "Are you okay?" he asked and took over wrist duty.

To Lauren's surprise, exhilaration exploded somewhere deep inside. "Better than I've been in a long time. I did something I never thought I could do, something significant. I didn't let him make me a victim. I feel great!"

The look he gave her screamed skepticism, but then he shrugged and turned his attention back to the man who'd wound up her victim instead of attacker. All of a sudden, he grinned.

"Well, well, well! How've you been, Theodosius Bentley Witherspoon? Long time no see. Looks like all the bail you posted the last time you attacked Lauren's going to be gone for good."

A stream of curses followed, courtesy of

Theodosius.

Lauren glared at her two-time attacker.

The old ladies objected — loudly.

"For shame!" one cried.

"Only the ignorant resort to obscenities, you know," another stated.

The beehive-haired body-slammer ventured, "He must've been traumatized as a child. He needs counseling."

"Traumatized?" Grandma Dottie argued. "Gimme a break, Ophelia. Don't go giving slime like this any more excuses to avoid accountability."

"Whoo-eee! Lookit what I got." A fifth one waved what looked like a dead animal over her head. "A souvenir!"

"Gross!"

"Drop it, Melba. Who knows what kind of creepy-crawlies are in it?"

"Not on your life. I snatched it off his head. It's *my* trophy. Find your own. Check to see if he's got dentures or something."

Lauren got a better look at the molting pelt, and then laughed out loud. "It's a wig! We caught a vain crook. Way to go, ladies."

Ophelia winked at Lauren and grinned. "How appropriate. I'm a professional beauty expert. Vanity is my thing. I sell Lady Look Lovely cosmetics." She stepped back, squinted, and studied Lauren. "I could work

wonders on you, honey. Let's get together
—"

"Oh, no you don't, Ophelia Simmons,"
David cut in. "Lauren's gorgeous just the
way she is. Don't you go drafting her into
your makeup parties. You've got enough
victims as it is."

Gorgeous? Nobody'd ever called her gorgeous before.

"Watch it, Davey!" the makeup peddler
warned. "Your grandma will have something
to say about your comments."

"Yeah," Grandma Dottie said. "Get to
work, and stick this creep back in a cage
where he belongs."

David tipped his head toward his grandmother. "Aye, aye, Captain." He stood and
yanked Theodosius up by the handcuffs.
"What do you say, Theo? You missed all that
gourmet jailhouse cuisine, didn't you? You
really did work hard to get back in the chow
line."

"Don't call me Theo! That's not my name.
It's Theodosius, a fine name with a long history of honorable men who've worn it."

"Yeah, yeah, yeah," David said. "It's still a
mouthful for a small-potatoes crook."

Theodosius shrugged his mountainous
shoulders, causing an earthquake under the
expensive-looking coat. "I'll have you know,

I'm no small-potatoes. I've pulled off big
—"

"Wait!" Lauren cried, cutting off his potential confession and, more importantly, stopping the cop-and-crook parade toward the door. "Hold on. He dropped something."

She bent over to pick up a shiny, rectangular gold charm. The piece measured one inch wide by two and a half long. It displayed a stylized bird in relief, its appearance foreign in flavor, but familiar nonetheless.

"David!" she called. "Take a look at this."

A police officer took hold of the arm David had held so he could come to Lauren's side. She held out the gold piece.

He took it, turned it over and over again, studied the symbol then met her gaze. "What is it?"

"What do you mean, what is it? It's a bird, it's a plane . . . David! Aloysius — remember the now-dead birdman? — came looking for a bird. Do I have to connect the dots for you?"

"I can see it's a bird, and I didn't forget the bird issue, but I don't know what this particular item might be. What does it mean? What is it for? Do you know?"

She shook her head. "But I have seen a

similar one. Ric had it on his key chain."

"Really?" David stared at the strange object some more. "These marks look like hieroglyphics. Are they the real deal or just some kind of bogus decoration? Do you know what they might mean?"

"I've told you Ric had almost no contact with Mark and me. When would he have found the time to tell me all about a snazzy key chain?"

He met her gaze. "I know and you know that if this character's got the same kind of bauble your brother carried, then it's more than just a key chain."

"Obviously." Then something occurred to her. "Did you guys find another one on . . ." She shuddered. "On Aloysius?"

"I don't know. I only read the police catalog of his personal belongings. I didn't go through the stuff myself, but I'll let you know what I learn when I check out what's in the box in the evidence room."

"Thanks."

He reached out and touched the spot on her cheek where he'd dried her tear on Christmas Eve. "A promise is a promise. Remember that. You *can* trust me."

Lauren fought the urge to clasp his hand. Even more, she had to fight the spontaneous impulse to tell him she did trust him.

But something held her back. She had to be sure nothing would ever hurt Mark. And their troubles weren't over yet. David figured prominently in all that happened since her brother's death. Until she knew beyond a doubt he'd had nothing to do with the weird mess, she couldn't let herself trust him. If then.

"Please call me when you know," was all she said.

He held her gaze a moment longer, then nodded and walked away. Lauren stayed in place, watched him go.

An arm curved around her shoulders. "Give him a chance," Grandma Dottie said. "David's as honest and trustworthy a man as our Father in heaven has ever created. If there's even a glimmer of success, he'll keep you and Mark safe."

Then Lauren remembered the most important, most critical detail of the attempted kidnapping. How could she have let it slip her mind? She turned to Grandma Dottie.

"Please take my shopping bag and purse. I have to catch up to David."

She took off, ran down toward the exterior doors through which David, the police and their captive had exited. She nearly stumbled on them on the sidewalk. David stood to one side while officers loaded the argumentative Theodosius into the patrol car.

"There you are!" She paused to catch her breath.

David turned, fear in his face. "What happened? Are you okay? Is Gram all right? What's wrong?"

She waved and drew another deep breath. "I'm fine . . . she's fine. But I remembered something . . . something you need to know."

He placed his hands on her shoulders. "What is it?"

Lauren welcomed his strength and support, even though she knew she shouldn't. "Mark! He wanted Mark."

"Mark? Are you sure? What did he say?"

"Of course, I'm sure. He told me to go with him, to lead him to Mark."

"That doesn't make sense. What would he want with Mark?"

Lauren glared. "Don't ask me for more answers I don't have! Do your job. Figure it out, then come and let me know."

"Oh, I will. I'll figure it out, all right. Then I'll come back and let you know." He gave her shoulders a gentle squeeze. "You can count on me."

She didn't respond.

He walked away.

EIGHTEEN

"Who would do such a thing?" Grandma Dottie asked when they'd returned to her home.

Lauren stared at the fragments of plastic and metal that once were Ochiban, Mark's most prized possession. Tears scalded her eyes; rage burned in her gut.

"Someone without a heart." She fought to contain her anger. "Someone who belongs in jail next to Theodosius, if Theodosius didn't do it himself."

Mark sobbed against her chest. "But Daddy gave him to me."

She understood his pain. The little robot had been Ric's last gift to his son. That gift had been the last tangible link between a boy and the father he'd just lost.

"Humph!" Grandma Dottie smacked the wall with her open palm. "It just gives me the willies to think some sick animal got in the house while we were gone. What if Bea had come here to watch the boy?"

She didn't need to say anything more. Lauren's imagination filled in the blanks. Instead of a robot, Mark could have been at the receiving end of the intruder's wrath. She tightened her hold on his warm, vibrant body.

"Did you call —"

"I'm on my way," Grandma Dottie said.

Lauren made a face. "Calling cops has become a routine thing for me lately. I'm so ready to break out of this routine."

Grandma Dottie said, "I hear you."

Mark sniffled. "Will the cops catch the guy who killed Ochiban?"

Lauren's heart ached for him. "I'm sure they will." She smoothed her hand over his dark hair. "Let's go wash your face so you can help the police find the bad guy."

Mark's eyes opened wide. "You mean I can? Really?"

"I'll bet they'll come with a bunch of important questions for you. You have to answer everything as well as you can."

"Is it gonna be hard?"

"No, honey. Just take your time to think about the questions they ask, and then do your best to tell them everything you know. That's it, nothing more."

David walked in when Lauren had dried

Mark's tears. The boy ran into the man's open arms. Mark hugged David's neck and his legs clamped David's middle. David cupped the back of the boy's head, held him close to his chest and met Lauren's gaze. "All of you okay?"

She nodded. "There's our only victim."

David's anger caught Lauren by surprise. Rage burned in his eyes. His lips turned into a thin, white-edged line. His jaw reminded her of hewn granite, and his stance was that of a lion ready to pounce.

"He won't get away with terrorizing two women and a child."

"I'm not terrorized as much as I'm angry," she said.

He met her gaze. "Good. I'm going to need you to think through everything, nothing's insignificant. Just concentrate on the details. This won't stop until we come up with that missing link. And I don't think it's something that stares us in the face."

She appreciated the "we" in his analysis. "It's probably something we've looked at a million times, but somehow managed to miss its significance."

David went to talk to the officers who'd just arrived, and Lauren, with Mark in her arms, returned to Grandma Dottie's side. The police handled the little boy with compassion and sensitivity. Lauren had the distinct feeling they viewed the perpetrator with the same contempt as David did.

When the police finally left, the Lathams, Lauren and Mark went for a late-afternoon lunch to a popular Chinese restaurant. There, they made plans for the next few days, and eventually came around to the subject of New Year's Eve and Day. Everyone agreed to spend New Year's Eve at home with some of Grandma Dottie's kooky friends who had no family nearby. Then they got around to New Year's Day.

"No way are you and Mark going to that parade," David stated.

Lauren glared. "We've done this all our lives, and we're not about to stop now."

"So what if you've gone all your lives? So have I, but this year's different. You've both been threatened. I'm responsible for your safety, and I say you can't go."

"I'm responsible for keeping Mark's memory of his father alive, and we're going."

"No, you're not."

"Yes, we are."

Lauren refused to argue further, so she turned to Grandma Dottie, and asked about the Lady Look Lovely women who would join them in a few days to usher in the new year. David took the hint, but his stony expression didn't budge.

Two days later, David walked into the house, a grim expression on his face, a determined set to his shoulders. He covered the newspaper want ads Lauren had spread over the kitchen table with a sheaf of papers.

"There's a link," he said. "It might not be *the* link, but we've connected some dots."

Lauren picked up the papers one by one. She first saw a rubbing of the bird and hieroglyphics she'd identified on Theodosius's gold piece. The next paper contained a quote from some research source. She began to read.

". . . its connection with rebirth came to associate it also with Osiris. In quoting from the Book of the Dead, Wallis Budge quotes a passage that reads, 'I go in like the Hawk, and I come forth like the Bennu, the Morning Star (i.e., the planet Venus) of Ra; I am the Bennu which is in Heliopolis' and he goes on to say that the scholion on this passage expressly informs us that the Bennu is Osiris. In essence, the Bennu was considered a manifestation of the resurrected Osiris."

"This reads like a high school lecture on

Egyptian mythology," she said, confused. "What does this have to do with anything? With the bird?"

"If you'll read further, you'll see that neo-pagans incorporate ancient mythology into beliefs and practices. One of the sources is Egyptian mythology."

She shuddered. "Are you telling me that this bird is Bennu, an Egyptian god?"

"That seems to be the case. We found another gold piece among Aloysius's belongings."

"Do you think the gold cards . . . charms . . . whatever they are, identify members of some particular group of pagans?"

"That's what J.Z. and I think."

"Can you imagine how hard it is to hear that? To try and make that click with the Ric I grew up with?"

"Can you imagine how hard it was for me to come to tell you something I knew would hurt?"

She met his gaze, and what she saw there caused her heart to flutter. He seemed so sincere, so caring. She wished she could trust him, that she could — No! That kind of thought led to a trap that would crush more than the kind made for animals in the wild.

Her shrug seemed to bother him.

But he continued without any mention of the gesture. "You may be angry with God right now, just as I know you resent me for doing my job, but I know that deep inside you love the Father, that the faith your family shared with you is at the core of who Lauren DiStefano is."

"But —"

"God didn't betray you. I didn't betray you. And even though I understand why you feel that way, your brother didn't betray you. He betrayed God. He turned his back on the Lord, and followed a false religion. He lost his way."

"I agree. Ric did betray God, but he also betrayed his son and me. The choices he made didn't take our safety, and especially his son's future, into consideration."

"Leave it with God. Trust Him to heal your hurt."

His warm gaze felt like a powerful invitation. She wanted to accept it, even though she wasn't certain where the invitation would lead. After all the upheaval she'd experienced, she wanted assurances, something she could cling to. Right now, she could only count on herself.

"I can't," she whispered.

"Yes, you can, and you can trust me, too."

He reached out and took her hand. "But you'll have to look beyond what you feel. You'll have to look to the Cross, and then step out in faith."

Tears welled up in her eyes. A deep, powerful yearning burned inside her. But her fear was greater still. She couldn't overcome it. She shook her head.

"At least promise me you won't go to the parade. It's obvious you and Mark are in someone's sights — someone with ties to your brother. I can't be everywhere on that street. Please stay here where I can have constant surveillance, where I know you'll both be safe."

"I can't, David. I can't give in. If I do that, they — whoever they are — will win. Mark needs to be at the parade, if for no other reason, than as a final goodbye to Ric."

He clamped his lips in disapproval. "Your stubbornness could lead to his final goodbye period. Yours, too."

"So be it." She raised her chin. "And you ask me to trust the God who would allow that . . ."

She refused to continue the disagreement. She also refused to revisit it the various times he tried to bring it up, which was whenever he stopped by his grandmother's house. That's why, on New Year's Day, she dressed in her warmest clothes, bundled Mark up and called a cab. Even inside the closed vehicle, she could hear the excitement of the crowd. She could also hear strains of street band music.

She missed the old days, her childhood and her family, more than ever.

"This is *fun!*" Mark cried as they made their way to the curb. "I wish Monster Man'd come with us."

"Me —" Lauren caught herself. How had it happened? From arguing over the event, she'd come to where she wished she could share the day with David.

She conceded she liked him more than she should. And given a different set of circumstances, she might have cared much more for him, more than just *like*. But she couldn't. Not now, not after everything had gone wrong in her life.

All she could hope for was his presence on the street. He'd promised he'd be there, with J.Z. and a group of other agents, to try and make sure she and Mark survived the parade. For some reason, he believed their lives were still at risk, even with Aloysius dead and Theodosius behind bars.

He insisted Ochiban's hard drive, stolen by the robot's "killer," proved that danger still existed. Lauren felt the danger was over, the thief had what he wanted. Why he would want a toy's operating system remained a mystery, but at least he had what he'd wanted.

Lauren couldn't understand his concern for them out on the street, either. They'd be in broad daylight, in the middle of a throng of paradegoers. Would anyone be so stupid as to attack her or Mark with that many witnesses around them? She didn't think so.

With that in mind, she sat on the edge of the curb, pulled Mark into her lap, and let herself enjoy the colorful pageantry and cheery music that gave the Mummer's and Shooter's parade its flavor. She forced all thought of the dark underbelly of the activity's roots, the fascination with pagan idolatry and all that meant out of her mind.

When the Fancy Clubs began to make their way up the street, she experienced a pang of grief. Ric would have been among his friends out there, laughing and playing to the crowd just like the rest of the men in their outrageous costumes.

Mark's thoughts must have run along the same lines. "Daddy had a cool costume."

She thought back to the day Don came for the finished piece of the outfit. "Well, your uncle Don's out there in your daddy's costume. Let's see if we can pick him out."

Before long, Ric's club made its way toward them. Lauren spotted Don right away. Like the others in the club, he wore a spectacular yellow, green and red costume reminiscent of an Amazonian parrot. The one thing that didn't match the bird's familiar look was the enormous sunlike headdress the men wore. Yellow feathers radiated from the head out to about three feet and ended in more feathers, these a fiery red. The bodices were iridescent pieces of fabric art, with their millions of hand-sewn sequins. The yellow of the headdress continued on the front of the shirt, but then the sides turned orange and the backs matched the feathers on the perimeter of the headdresses. The pants were shimmery green, the sequins sparkling in the winter-morning sunshine.

And then she saw him. At the end of the back row.

"Ric . . . ?"

Before she could stop him, Mark flew off her lap and ran. "Daddy!"

Ric's made-up face burst into a mile-wide smile. He scooped up his son in his arms, and spun away from the rest of the men. Lauren rose and followed her brother and nephew. But Ric had no intention of letting her catch up.

He bolted. Over the music, the noise of the spectators and her blood pounding in her ears, Lauren still heard Mark cry, "Aunt Lauren! Come with us."

She didn't need an invitation, but Ric ran faster than she could in spite of the unwieldy feather-and-wire contraption on his head. Still, she refused to give up. "Stop! Wait, Ric. Hold on."

People on either side gave her a wide berth. She suspected she looked like a mad-woman, chasing a gargantuan bird with a child in his arms, but she had no alternative. She had to catch up with them; she had a litany of questions, she needed to know why Ric had gone through such an elaborate farce and faked his death.

She feared she already knew why.

"Stop!" she yelled again. When her brother showed no intention of slowing down, she changed her cry. "Stop him, someone! He's taking my nephew."

The crowd parted and, instead of holding him, gave Ric the chance to slip away. But he must not have realized where he was. When Lauren followed, she saw him at the end of an alley, panting, Mark still in his arms.

"Why?" she asked as she ran up.

"None of your business," he countered.

"But if you want to help me and Mark, you'll hurry up and come with us. Help me get away from here."

"Where do you want to go? Why did you make me think you'd died? Why did you try to run me over? What is this all about?"

"I'll tell you when we're on the plane."

"Plane! Where are you going?"

"Mark and I are going somewhere safe. Right, buddy? Daddy's taking you on an adventure."

Instead of excitement, Mark's face showed confusion and some fear. "Where we going, Daddy?"

"Don't ask," Ric said, agitated. His head-dress quivered all the way to the red tips as he looked from side to side. "If you don't want me to really die, Lauren, you'll help me get away."

"So it's true. You did help the mob."

"You don't know anything about anything. You were always too naive for your own good. Now you just have two choices. You can help me get away in one piece, or you can be responsible for my arrest . . . or my death."

"That's right, DiStefano," David called from the mouth of the alley. "It's either jail or a bullet. If you're as smart as you're supposed to be, you'll choose jail. At least that way you can see your son grow into the man you, too, should have been."

Ric's eyes went wild. "I'm not going down."

Lauren looked at her brother. The love she'd always had for him urged her to help him, even though he'd brought disaster on himself through his criminal choices. Family loyalty lived strong and deep inside her.

Then she looked at David. Her gaze met his, and something in those hazel eyes led her to an epiphany. She'd tried to tell herself she hated him, that he was responsible for some if not all that had happened to her, that only if they'd met under different circumstances she could have cared for him, maybe even loved the intense, driven federal agent.

But now she had to face the truth. She did care for David. And she had no idea how it had happened. She just knew that he stood before her, asking her brother to do the right but difficult thing. Her brother refused.

"I'm not alone, you know," Ric said. "I have friends who're coming to help me. And you're just one man."

David smiled. "Keep on thinking that. But I have friends, too. And they're on the right side of the law. They have my back."

Another bird stumbled up behind David. "Come on, Ric," he yelled. "I have a gun on him. He won't get a shot off before I plug him."

Lauren's horror grew. "Don! Are you crazy? What are you doing? What is wrong with you and Ric?"

Mark began to cry. "Don't hurt Monster Man!"

"Great," Ric said. "You've brainwashed my son. Now he's sticking up for your boyfriend. What kind of sister are you?"

"The kind who's been betrayed by the brother she loved, Ric. Think about it. You pretended to die, you tried to kill me with a car, you had my windows shot out, and you even had Ochiban destroyed. You hurt Mark and me, so don't try to displace your guilt onto me."

David stood rock-still, too aware of the weapon aimed at him. Lauren's heart ached. He might die because of her.

On the other hand, her brother stood in the same situation.

What could she do? How should she respond?

David must have understood her feelings; he must have come to know her well enough to read her better than anyone ever had. "Don't let him do this to you, Lauren.

302

Trust, that's what it's all about. Not his threats or their crimes."

She looked from man to man. Emotions warred inside her.

She'd always treasured her family. But if she let that loyalty win, she'd leave Don to threaten and maybe kill David while she helped her brother escape. She'd have to go with him because he had Mark, with no plans to let the boy go. She couldn't give up the little boy she loved like her own.

Or she could do what her every instinct told her was legal, moral, ethical and the right thing to do. She could somehow distract the men so that David could turn on Don, disarm him, and hold him at bay. Hopefully she could trust the rest of the FBI agents would show up in time to capture Ric.

In either case, bullets were sure to fly. Mark was in the line of fire. Fear choked her. Her stomach clenched. Pain swelled in her chest, a physical ache unlike anything she'd ever felt before.

"Trust, Lauren," David said again. "You know how to do it. Don't turn your back on God this time. He's here. He's on our side. Trust Him. I do."

Ric laughed a nasty laugh. "Oh, sure, Lauren. Go back to Dad's mumbo-jumbo junk.

Like some bearded old guy in heaven's going to listen to you and bail you out."

Lauren took her gaze from David and studied her brother. His harsh words wore an edge of cynicism she'd never heard him express. He had sold out to his pagan tradition. But in his eyes, fear burned hot.

And that fear spoke volumes to her. His idols were empty; they gave Ric nothing to hold on to. He had to trust Don, their Mummer pals and some goofy Egyptian bird symbol for protection or salvation.

In David's eyes she saw faith, assurance and love. Once, she'd felt that way about whatever life might bring her way. But she'd come face-to-face with a kind of evil she'd never imagined — and at the hand of the brother she'd loved, still loved but couldn't support. She could never help a criminal escape.

What could she do?

Mark sobbed.

"Come on, Lauren," Ric said in that wild, hard voice. "I gotta get going or they'll turn me into target practice."

"Come stand by me," David said, his voice calm and gentle. "With God's help we'll get through this."

"Aunt Lauren, please . . ." Mark's eyes begged, but she didn't know what he wanted from her. He seemed unable to put into words what he felt in his heart.

Three different directions; three different ways to turn. Which was right?

She looked back at David. His eyes reflected his faith in God the Father, His Son and Holy Spirit. They also held something else. Unless she was much mistaken, a wealth of emotion shone there for her, a treasure she could tap into if only . . .

If only she stepped out in faith and trust.

A flash of understanding hit her. When seen in comparison to the two costumed men, David looked tiny, defenseless. The massive headdresses gave Ric and Don the illusion of strength and power. But their fear betrayed that appearance.

David's faith gave him true strength. Like the David who confronted Goliath and won, armed only with an insignificant slingshot and faith in God, David knew victory.

She had a decision to make. Would she choose her past and the false strength Ric offered or would she choose the future based on God's power and might?

A future with David in it, too.

She shivered. *Oh, Lord. I'm scared. I've felt so alone, so abandoned. Were You there? Are You here? Will You see us through?*

The simple act of prayer, disjointed as it

was, eased the shaking in her hands. She kept her gaze on David, bolstered by his love, trust and faith in the Father and encouragement for her.

She took a step toward him.

"Don't leave me!" Panic shrilled Mark's voice. "Aunt Lauren, pleeeze . . . Daddy's scaring me."

Before she turned to the child, the rage David wore when she showed him Ochiban's remains returned. His anger wasn't aimed at her or at Mark. It was for the man who cared so little for his son that instead of the love, protection and guidance God showed his children, he offered only fear, pain and possible injury.

In that moment she knew what she had to do. She had to trust God and step forward in faith. She turned to her brother and held out her arms.

"Give him to me, Ric. Look what you're doing to him. That's as criminal as the dirty money you accumulated and whatever else you've done in your secret life."

He barked another of those harsh laughs. "Are you nuts? I'm not handing him over. He's my ticket out. Your boyfriend's not going to shoot me as long as I hold Mark. Just watch me leave."

He took three steps forward.

A familiar voice yelled, "Now!"

Ric faltered.

She yanked Mark out of his grasp.

David turned on Don.

A shower of bullets rained down.

Don was hit, he screamed, and bled . . . green?

Ric's blood came out purple.

Even David flinched from a strike. He spurted yellow blood.

"Woo-hoo!" Ophelia of the weird hair color cheered. "I got the creep with the gun."

"That's nothing," Bea crowed. "I got the slimeball who tried to run over Lauren. He's the one who wants to run off with our baby."

"Hey, I got Davey." Grandma Dottie shook her head. "What were you thinking? You should've sat with Lauren and Mark to watch the parade, not hung out with your missing-in-action spooks."

"So where are Davey's spooks?" Melba asked.

"Okay, ladies," J.Z. said, a rare touch of humor in his deep voice. "You can put down your weapons. We had them covered the whole time. I will say, though, your aim is impressive."

Lauren hugged Mark close then turned to see another nonuniformed man clap handcuffs on Don's wrists. A look out the corner of her eye showed her another one fitting her brother with bracelets of his own.

Ophelia turned on J.Z. "Oh, yeah, sure. You had 'em covered all right. So why'd you let Lauren and our Mark sweat bullets if you were watching these animals? Huh? If we Lady Look Lovely women hadn't come to their rescue they'd still be stuck arguing with the creeps."

An arm surrounded Lauren's shoulders. "Are you okay?"

"We sure are, Monster Man! That was awesome." Mark lowered his head for a moment. "Well, it was scary, too."

Lauren met David's gaze over the boy's head. "You have his answer."

"How about yours?"

The question came with layers of meaning. She gave him a slow, warm smile. "I am now."

His hold tightened as he drew her closer against his side. "Thank the Lord."

A tear rolled down her cheek. "Better late than never, but Amen to that."

This time, instead of drying the drop with his finger, David used his lips. Lauren felt the caress burrow all the way into her heart. She gave herself up to the tenderness of the moment, and leaned on David's solid strength.

"After I'm done with all the official stuff," he murmured, "you and I have a date."

She nodded. "We have a lot to talk about."

"A lot."

"C'n I come talk, too?"

David took Mark from Lauren's arms and sat him on his shoulders. "Not this time, pal. This time Aunt Lauren and I have grown-up stuff to settle."

"Oh," Mark said, disgusted. "You're gonna kiss her again. I don't like mushy stuff. No more bullets, huh?"

Grandma Dottie marched up and showed him her weapon. "Not them, kiddo. They're boring. You can come and watch us practice with our paint-guns. Now that's an awesome deal."

Mark giggled.

David chuckled.

Lauren groaned into his sturdy shoulder.

"We've got our work cut out for us," David said.

She looked up. "For *us.*"

He gave her a gentle squeeze. "Later."

He released her, and again looked every inch the agent he could never not be. But this time, Lauren understood. And she'd tell him.

Later.

Epilogue

And later came, full of God's love, blessings and peace. The new year brought the pain of Ric's prosecution, but it also brought her something she'd never experienced before. With each day that went by, Lauren felt the Lord's strength uphold her through the tough moments, comfort her in the sad ones, and uplift her in the joy-filled ones.

Each day she fell more in love with David. They spent every possible minute together — just the two of them.

David's concepts of dates proved inventive and original. He took Lauren and Mark to a kite-making seminar, and Lauren found herself challenged and fascinated by the whimsical toys. She began to study the art in earnest, and was beginning to see the glimmer of a possible new career.

Another date took them to a golden retriever rescue center. Needless to say, Mark walked out with a brand-new family member. Naming the once-abandoned puppy took a bit of patience and understanding — on all sides.

"Yes, Mark, retrievers do fetch," she said. "They were bred to retrieve hunters' prey."

"Yuck!" the boy responded. "That sounds bloody and yucky. But that means Fetch is the perfect name for 'im."

She frowned. "That's almost as bad as if you'd been named Growing Boy. Let's try something else."

He didn't answer right away, and Lauren could almost see the wheels turn inside his head. At her side, she felt the silent chuckles of Mark's "bestest friend," the Monster Man. She shot the overgrown kid a look of exasperation.

"You know," Mark then said, "if I can't call 'im Fetch, then I can't call Grandma Dottie Grandma. That's what she does, you know. She *is* a grandma."

"He's got you there," David whispered in her ear.

"Do we really have to name the poor dog Fetch?" she asked, a plea in her voice.

"Why not? It's unique, and I think it's cute." At Lauren's grimace, David chuckled. "Besides, he *is* Mark's dog."

Lauren gritted her teeth, counted to ten, and when no further argument came to her, she capitulated. "Okay, Mark. Fetch it is."

With every experience, Lauren realized that they were building something precious between the three of them. And when she and David went on "just the two of us, Mark" dates, her happiness mixed in with the sheer excitement of spending time with the man she loved.

He could make a simple dinner at a restaurant a special occasion. And the night they planned to eat at a French place that featured a violinist who serenaded patrons at tableside, Lauren couldn't wait.

She wore a mint-green silk dress and took special care when she applied her makeup. Then David arrived, and his eyes lit up with admiration. Hers did the same. He looked elegant, distinguished even, in his gray suit.

Dinner lived up to the restaurant's excellent reputation. And the company, of course, was perfect. David had just closed another case, and could now share with Lauren some of the details. His enthusiasm always captured her attention and carried her along.

But when the strawberry-and-cream pastry dessert arrived, accompanied by the violinist, Lauren found herself speechless. She stared at the clouds of cream, the red berries, the crystal plate, and tears rolled down her cheeks. For there, at the very top of the white billows, perched the most exquisite diamond ring she'd ever seen.

She looked at David, and the rest of the world fell away. Only the two of them and the sweet notes of the violin existed right then.

"Will you marry me?" he asked.

"Oh, David . . . yes! Yes, yes, yes!"

The time that followed came full of joy and even more excitement. Lauren and Grandma Dottie began to plan a small but beautiful wedding, and Mark told everyone who would listen that he was getting a Monster Man Daddy-2. Somehow, he had managed to disassociate the horror of Ric's current situation from the father he loved. At the same time, he realized that David was a man he could trust, a father that wouldn't let him down.

And Lauren's renewed faith in her heavenly Father grew, deepened. Her gratitude knew no bounds. God's bounty left her breathless, as He graced her with a new family to treasure, a man to love and trust, one totally hers and totally God's.

David, a godly man, another man after God's heart, one who had offered himself

as an instrument of the Father's righteousness.

The love of her life.

Dear Reader,

As the mother of four boys, I've had many chances to think about the Lord's sense of humor. I mean, really. Four? Plus all their assorted friends — of the male persuasion, of course. And me from a family of two girls.

When things get too crazy, troubles hit too close to home, or I just need a time-out, I've always reached for satisfying reads that make me smile . . . or howl with laughter, as the case may be. After that form of refreshment, I'm again ready to face life with the sense of humor the Lord gives us fully restored.

The opportunity Steeple Hill has given me to share my offbeat stories with you is a blessing I treasure. I pray the faith of my characters will reinforce your own. To me, that is a *book*. Thanks for giving my *book* room in your heart.

Blessings,
Ginny Aiken

QUESTIONS FOR DISCUSSION

1. Lauren claims that her late brother, Ric, tried to run her and her nephew down on the street in front of her house. David wants to believe her, but her story is slightly far-fetched. If you were David, would you believe her? Why or why not?

2. Eliza, David's boss, is somewhat difficult to work for. Have you ever had to deal with a less-than-ideal boss? What did you do to make the working relationship better?

3. After her sister-in-law's death, Lauren put her teaching career on hold to take care of her brother and nephew. Have you or anyone you know ever had to give up something you cared about deeply to help someone else?

4. Lauren's brother, Ric, kept many secrets

from her and her nephew, Mark, which put their lives in jeopardy. Could Lauren have done more to find out about Ric's secret life? If so, what?

5. It is often said, no man is an island. David relies on his friends J.Z. and Dan to help him solve Lauren's case. Do you have good friends you can rely on in troubled times? Can they also turn to you in times of need?

6. David is very close to his grandmother, Grandma Dottie, chauffeuring her around town, staying over at her house, talking to her often. How did you get along with your grandparents? Were they as active as Dottie and her friends? If they are no longer around, what do you miss about them most?

7. When Lauren meets David's friend, Walker Hopkins, based on his appearance she assumes that's he's a bodyguard or a bouncer, rather than an accountant. Are we all guilty of judging people by their outward appearance? How can we prevent ourselves from doing so?

8. While David and his friends all walk

closely with God, Lauren's faith is tested during the book. Do you agree with Walker that Lauren needs to find her own way back to God, or with David, who wants to help her? Have you ever been in a similar situation? How so?

9. Lauren's brother, Ric, sought out witchcraft as a way to fill his life after his wife's death. Have you ever been tempted to stray from God's love? If so, how did you find your way back?

10. For Lauren and David, Christmas Eve is a gift of calm in the middle of her stormy life. What is a typical Christmas Eve like for you and your family? Calm or stormy? Please describe.

ABOUT THE AUTHOR

Ginny Aiken, a former newspaper reporter, lives in Pennsylvania with her engineer husband and their three younger sons — the oldest married and flew the coop. Born in Havana, Cuba, raised in Valencia and Caracas, Venezuela, she discovered books early, and wrote her first novel at age fifteen while she trained with the Ballets de Caracas, later known as the Venezuelan National Ballet. She burned that tome when she turned a "mature" sixteen. Stints as reporter, paralegal, choreographer, language teacher and retail salesperson followed. Her life as wife, mother of four boys and herder of their numerous and assorted friends, brought her back to books and writing in search of her sanity. She's now the author of twenty-one published works, a frequent speaker at Christian women's and writer's workshops, but has yet to catch up with that elusive sanity.

The employees of Thorndike Press hope you have enjoyed this Large Print book. All our Thorndike and Wheeler Large Print titles are designed for easy reading, and all our books are made to last. Other Thorndike Press Large Print books are available at your library, through selected bookstores, or directly from us.

For information about titles, please call:
(800) 223-1244

or visit our Web site at:
http://gale.cengage.com/thorndike

To share your comments, please write:
Publisher
Thorndike Press
295 Kennedy Memorial Drive
Waterville, ME 04901